WRON

'Did either of you hear the phone ring?'
Peter said.

'It did,' said Miranda. 'I answered it. It
was a man. He didn't say who he was.'

Peter looked annoyed. 'You didn't ask?'

'I didn't get a chance to ask,' said
Miranda. 'He started talking straight
away. Anyway, it must have been a
wrong number.'

'How do you know? Miranda, my
dad won't be pleased if I've missed an
important message.'

'You haven't. I'm sure it was a wrong
number. What he said didn't make any
sense at all. "Falcon delivery confirmed.
Friday at three. Top floor, as usual." '

'Falcon?' said Holly.

'What else did he say?' asked Peter.

'Nothing,' said Miranda. 'That was it.
Then he hung up.'

The Mystery Kids series

THE MYSTERY KiDS

Wrong Number

Fiona Kelly

Hodder
Children's
Books

a division of Hodder Headline plc

Special thanks to Michael Coleman

Copyright © 1996 Ben M. Baglio
Created by Ben M. Baglio
London W6 0HE

First published in Great Britain in 1996
by Hodder Children's Books

A Catalogue record for this book is
available from the British Library

ISBN 0 340 65566 6

Typeset by Hewer Text Composition Services, Edinburgh
Printed and bound in Great Britain by
Cox & Wyman Ltd, Reading, Berks

Hodder Children's Books
a division of Hodder Headline plc
338 Euston Road
London NW1 3BH

Contents

Breakdown!

'Miss Adams?' said the serious-looking figure standing on the doorstep.

'Yes.'

'Miss Holly Adams?'

Holly nodded, her shoulder-length brown hair bouncing up and down as she did so. 'Yes,' she said again.

He turned to look at the girl standing at Holly's side.

'And you must be Miss Hunt?'

'Got it in one!'

'Miss Miranda Hunt.'

Miranda, Holly's best friend, stuck her thumb in the air. 'Right again.'

The figure on the doorstep looked at the two girls, his eyes moving from one to the other.

'Holly Adams and Miranda Hunt,' he said

finally, 'I must ask you to accompany me to the police station.'

'What, now?' said Miranda.

'But why!' said Holly.

'Because my dad's offered to give us a lift!' said Peter Hamilton, his face finally losing its serious look and breaking into a wide grin. 'Come on!'

'Thanks, Mr Hamilton,' said Holly, as she and Miranda climbed into the back seat.

'No problem,' said Mr Hamilton, turning round. 'I was going into town anyway. And the chance of delivering you three into the hands of the police was too good to miss!'

Holly, Miranda and Peter all laughed. The three of them were firm friends. They called themselves the Mystery Kids, because they enjoyed investigating anything to do with mysteries. Mystery books, mystery television programmes – and especially any mysterious goings-on they happened to stumble across!

Because of this – and because their snooping had often managed to solve real crimes – they'd been invited along for a tour of their local police station, in Highgate, North London, where they lived.

2

'They *are* going to let us out again, you know,' said Peter.

'Really?' said Mr Hamilton, pretending to look disappointed. 'You don't think you should ask if they'll let you stay in the cells for a little while just to see what it's like? For a couple of months, say?'

'Charming!' cried Miranda, giving one of her louder laughs – which, in Miranda's case, meant very loud.

'I doubt they'd be able to keep us in for long anyway,' said Holly. 'Miranda could demolish the police station walls with her laugh!'

The three friends chattered on happily as Mr Hamilton started his car and moved off down the road.

Peter turned round to face the girls, his brown hair flopping over his eyes as he did so. He moved it away with the back of his hand.

'I read a brilliant book the other day,' he said.

'Don't tell me,' said Holly, '*Harriet the Spy*.'

The Mystery Kids enjoyed comparing notes about books they'd read. *Harriet the Spy* was their all-time favourite. They'd each read it dozens of times.

'No, not this time,' said Peter. 'It was a mystery book, about this really clever bank clerk who gets kidnapped and dumped in a car boot—'

'And sold?' interrupted Miranda. 'At a car boot sale?'

'No,' said Peter. 'She got taken to a secret hideaway miles from anywhere.'

'Sounds good,' said Holly.

'It is,' said Peter. 'But the best bit is how she manages to tell the police where she's being kept. How do you think?'

Holly thought hard. 'She finds a map in the car boot and tracks their route on it?' she said. 'No, that wouldn't work. She wouldn't be able to see. The light in a car boot goes out when it's closed, doesn't it – like the light in a fridge.'

'No maps involved,' said Peter. 'What do you think, Miranda?'

'Got it!' said Miranda, snapping her fingers. 'The boot's got a hole in it and she's able to see where they're going.'

'What sort of cars have holes in their boots?' frowned Peter.

4

Miranda tapped on the door at her side. 'Cars that are dead rusty. Like this one.'

'Thank *you*, Miranda!' said Mr Hamilton loudly. 'This car may not look perfect, but it *is* reliable!'

Peter gave his father a sideways look. 'What did you say you're going to town for, Dad?' he asked innocently.

Mr Hamilton knew when he was beaten. 'All right, so I'm going to get a spare part for the car,' he said, smiling. 'But until recently Guppy has been reliable.'

'Guppy?' said Miranda.

'It's Dad's pet name for his car,' explained Peter. 'It comes from the three letters in the numberplate – GUP.'

'It's not short for "give up", then?' said Miranda.

As if hearing her, Mr Hamilton's car coughed and spluttered a bit, then speeded up again.

'Sounds like Guppy's very sensitive to insults,' said Holly. 'Better keep your voice down Miranda.' She turned back to Peter. 'So how did the bank clerk tell the police how to find her then?' she said.

'By giving them directions,' said Peter.

'Even though she couldn't see anything, she could feel it when the car went round a corner. She had a fantastic memory, so it was dead easy for her to memorise all the left and right turns!'

'What about distances between the turns?' asked Holly.

'Simple. She could tell whether the car was going fast or slow from the sound of the engine. So she just counted how many seconds went at whatever speed they were going. When she finally tricked her kidnappers into letting her use the phone she just reeled off a list of directions like, "twenty seconds, fast, then turn left," and that was it. Knowing where to start from, the police could work out where she was!'

Brilliant!' said Holly. 'I wonder if I could do it? Although I wouldn't fancy being locked up in a boot!'

'I know I couldn't,' said Miranda. 'The bank clerk in Peter's book had a fantastic memory, not one like a leaky bucket.'

Holly closed her eyes. Could she do it? Was it even possible, or just something the author had thought up for the book?

It definitely *was* possible. With her eyes tightly shut, Holly found she could easily tell whether they were turning right or left. If it was right she slid across the back seat and bumped into Miranda; if it was left she slid the other way and found the window handle digging into her ribs.

And as for judging speed, that wasn't difficult either, especially in Mr Hamilton's old car. Whenever it went faster it coughed more and rattled less, and whenever it slowed down it coughed less and rattled more.

The tricky bit was remembering it all! Fast and coughing, fifteen seconds, left. Slow and rattling, ten seconds, right.

Now slower. Still rattling – coughing as well, this time. Ten . . . fifteen . . . twenty seconds.

Well! That was another thing you could tell, Holly realised: when the car had stopped! As Mr Hamilton's car came to a halt with a final burst of coughing and spluttering, Holly jerked her eyes open.

'Hey, it works!' she said. 'Are we there?'

'No, we're not,' whispered Miranda. 'And

if it works, it's more than can be said for this car. I think it's just packed up!'

Already, Mr Hamilton was climbing out of the driver's seat to raise the bonnet of his car. Peter got out of the passenger side to join him in looking for the problem.

As Holly and Miranda sat patiently in the back, odd words came floating through the window.

'Carburettor . . . crankshaft . . . gearbox . . . transmission . . .'

Finally, with a shake of his head, they heard Mr Hamilton sigh. 'I don't know, Peter. I'll have to call a garage.'

'Sorry,' said Peter as the two girls got out. 'It looks like Guppy's broken down completely this time.'

'Never mind,' said Holly. 'The police station isn't far from here. We can walk it.'

'Run it, you mean,' said Miranda. 'We're ten minutes late already!'

Mr Hamilton put on the car's warning lights and clanged the bonnet shut.

'I am sorry,' he said as he came round the side, wiping his greasy hands. 'But if the garage people get here in time, and if they can get it going again, I'll meet you all outside the police station.'

'Fine,' said Peter. 'But don't worry, Dad. If you're not there, we'll walk back.'

'You're sure?' said Peter's father.

'No problem, Mr Hamilton,' laughed Miranda. 'Holly's memorised the way home!'

'Ah, there you are,' said Sergeant Hopgood as the Mystery Kids dashed breathlessly into the police station. 'I was just about ready to send out a search party to look for you three.'

'A breakdown van would have been better,' said Miranda.

'Uh?'

'My dad's car packed up on the way here,' explained Peter.

'Not on double yellow lines, I hope,' said Sergeant Hopgood seriously, before breaking into a laugh. 'Only joking,' he said. 'Now, where do you want to start?'

'The cells!' said Miranda at once.

'The control room,' said Holly. 'How about you, Peter?'

'Everything,' said Peter. 'But especially the

9

control room – and the cells,' he added as Miranda gave him a jab in the ribs.

Sergeant Hopgood smiled. 'Well, I think we can manage all that. How about starting with the cells and ending in the control room?'

The Mystery Kids nodded excitedly, then followed Sergeant Hopgood as he led them through a couple of doors and along a brightly lit corridor.

As he reached a grey door with a spy-hole in the front, he pulled a collection of keys from his pocket. They were hanging on a silver chain attached to his belt.

'Here we are,' said Sergeant Hopgood. 'One cell.'

He looked through the spy-hole in the door. 'Better not show you one that's occupied, had I?' he laughed.

He put a key in the lock and turned it. The heavy door swung open to reveal a small room containing just a wooden bench-like bed, and a table and chair.

'Well, what do you think?'

'Shouldn't it be all dark and gloomy?' said Miranda. 'With gruesome things hanging from the walls?'

Sergeant Hopgood frowned. 'What sort of gruesome things?'

'Skeletons in chains!' cried Miranda.

Holly squealed. 'Miranda! This is a police cell, not a dungeon!'

Peter had walked right inside the cell and was looking around. 'Even so, it can't be much fun being shut in here on your own,' he said.

Sergeant Hopgood shook his head seriously. 'No, it's not. Which is why it's a good idea not to do anything that will cause it to happen.'

Holly looked up at the cell's only window. It was small, and had iron bars in front of it.

'Has anybody ever escaped from here?'

'Not yet,' smiled Sergeant Hopgood. 'But then we've never tried locking John Raven in here for the night.'

The three friends looked at each other. Secret Agent John Raven was the hero of the television programme, *Spyglass*. It was the one programme they all watched without fail. And once they'd actually rescued Maurice Harty – the actor who plays John Raven – from a blackmail attempt.

'You mean you watch *Spyglass* too?' said

Holly, wondering how John Raven *would* escape from a cell like this. The three friends liked to compare notes after every episode, saying how they thought John Raven was going to escape from his latest predicament.

'Never miss it!' said Sergeant Hopgood cheerfully. 'And it's on tonight, remember. So I think we'd better get a move on, don't you?'

'Wow!' said Peter.

Sergeant Hopgood needn't have said, 'And this is the control room.' It was obvious.

Around the walls, television screens flickered. They weren't showing programmes but views of different parts of the locality. Every now and then the picture changed to show a different area, or perhaps a scene at a busy road junction.

'Is this where all the emergency calls come in?' asked Holly.

'That's right,' said Sergeant Hopgood. 'Clare and Jimmy are on duty here today.'

He nodded towards a policewoman and a policeman, both seated at a table. They each had headsets on, with tiny microphones reaching out in front of them. Clare had pushed her microphone aside, and was taking a welcome sip of coffee.

'And when a call does come in,' said Peter, 'you call a patrol car, or an officer on the beat, and get them to investigate?'

'Right,' said Sergeant Hopgood.

The Mystery Kids smiled. They'd had more than their share of patrol cars coming to their aid!

'Anything exciting going on at the moment?' asked Miranda. 'A decent robbery, maybe?'

Sergeant Hopgood had the answer given for him. At that moment, Clare put her cup down and pushed her microphone back into place. She spoke urgently into it.

'Calling all patrols. Be on the lookout for a maroon Hewlett Sapphire, registration November Three Seven One Roger Whisky Tango reported stolen at sixteen hundred hours.'

'A stolen car!' hissed Peter. 'Numberplate N371 RWT.'

Holly looked at Sergeant Hopgood. 'Is it?'

The sergeant nodded seriously. 'Yes, I'm afraid it is.' He looked at Clare. 'Another one?' he said.

The policewoman nodded, swinging her

tiny microphone to one side. 'The second this month, Sarge,' said Clare. 'That makes six already this year. And all expensive models.'

Next to her, Jimmy said, 'Looks like we're dealing with an organised gang of car thieves, Sarge. Who knows where they're going to strike next?'

'Hey!' said Miranda, looking at Holly and Peter. 'Guess what I'm thinking!'

Sergeant Hopgood interrupted her at once. 'If you're thinking of looking for a gang of car thieves – don't! Not even for a minute. Take my word for it, they'll be mean and dangerous people.'

'Is that what you were thinking, Miranda?' asked Holly.

'No, as a matter of fact, it wasn't,' said Miranda.

'Then what were you thinking?' asked Peter.

Miranda grinned. 'I was thinking that if there's one car in Highgate that's completely safe from that gang, Peter, it's your dad's!'

Wrong Number

'What do car thieves do with the cars they steal, anyway?' asked Miranda as they stood outside the police station after saying goodbye to Sergeant Hopgood.

'Sell them, I suppose,' said Holly. 'To people who don't know they're stolen.'

'Sometimes to people who *do* know they're stolen,' said Peter. 'Especially with expensive cars. People who want one and don't care where it comes from sometimes ask gangs to steal a particular type of car for them.'

Holly shook her head sadly. 'But that's awful.'

Suddenly, she had an idea. 'Hey, Miranda. Why don't we write something about this for *The Tom-tom*?'

The three friends all went to the same school, The Thomas Petheridge Comprehensive. *The*

Tom-tom was the name of the lower-school magazine that Holly and Miranda produced.

Holly wrote a mystery column for it, usually describing any good mystery books or television programmes they'd seen. Sometimes, though, they tried to write more serious pieces about what kids could do to help prevent crimes taking place.

'Maybe we could ask everybody to look out for stolen cars?' said Holly.

'How?' said Miranda. 'Stolen cars look the same as any other!'

'I – I'm not sure,' said Holly.

'We could ask Sergeant Hopgood for the numberplates of cars that have been reported stolen from round here,' suggested Peter. 'And ask everybody to look out for those.'

'And we could start with this one,' said Holly, flipping open the Mystery Kids notebook she'd brought with her. 'N371 RWT,' she said, reading the number she'd written down in the police station control room. 'A maroon Hewlett Sapphire.'

'Good thinking!' said Miranda. 'Who knows, it could end up with somebody having their stolen car returned to them.'

A wide smile spread across her face. 'And I've got the perfect headline for your article, Holly. "Wheel Meet Again"!'

Holly and Peter groaned.

'Now I know why you write the bad jokes column in *The Tom-tom*,' said Peter.

'Talking of bad jokes,' said Miranda, 'I can't see your dad's car anywhere, Peter.'

'No,' said Peter, looking up and down the road outside the police station. There was no sign of Mr Hamilton, nor of his car.

'Perhaps the garage couldn't fix it,' said Holly as they started walking home.

'Perhaps they towed it away,' said Miranda. 'You know, Peter, to one of those places where they put old cars into one end of a machine and they come out of the other end looking like an Oxo Cube.'

'Guppy's not *that* bad a car, Miranda!' said Peter.

'I'm afraid it is, Peter,' said a voice from behind them.

The three friends turned to see Peter's father running to catch them up. 'Worse, in fact,' he said as he reached them. 'The garage people think it almost certainly needs a new engine.'

'Why, what happened?' asked Peter.

'After you left me I called Whittingham's Garage,' said Mr Hamilton. 'They sent somebody out. But even he couldn't get the car started. In the end it had to be towed back to the garage so they could have a better look at it.'

'And they think it needs a new engine?' said Peter.

'Yes.'

'But that isn't as bad as needing a new car, is it Mr Hamilton?' asked Holly.

'As good as, Holly,' said Peter's father. 'A new engine would cost more than the rest of the car is worth.'

'So what are you going to do?' asked Peter.

'Well,' said Mr Hamilton. 'I have been thinking for a while that old Guppy wasn't going to last too much longer. So while I was at Whittingham's I had a look round at the cars they'd got for sale.'

'You mean . . .' said Peter, excitedly.

'You're going to buy a new car!' said Miranda. 'Wow, a real swish cruisemobile, as long as a bus with tinted windows so that

Peter can pretend he's a pop-star or a president or something! Right, Mr Hamilton?'

'Not quite, Miranda,' laughed Mr Hamilton. 'But I have decided to buy another car. Whittingham's happened to have a newer version of our old one for sale. They also offered me a very good price for Guppy, even though it's only good for scrap.'

'What did I say?' hooted Miranda. 'Oxo Cube!'

'That's why I'm here,' continued Mr Hamilton. 'I've just finished a test drive and they dropped me off in town.'

'So, where is it?' asked Holly, looking around.

'Back at Whittingham's by now I should think,' said Mr Hamilton. 'It needs to be got ready and the paperwork sorted out. With luck, we'll have it in a couple of days!'

'We didn't see any swish cruisemobiles outside,' said Miranda as Peter answered his front door to them a couple of days later.

'Not so much as a tinted window,' said Holly. 'Where's the new car, Peter?'

'The garage haven't called yet,' said Peter

as the two girls piled into the hallway and he closed the door. 'But my dad said it could be any time today.'

'I bet you can hardly wait,' said Holly.

'Of course he can't,' laughed Miranda. 'It's not just a new car he's getting, Holly. It's a new numberplate for his collection as well!'

Peter smiled. Collecting car numberplates was his hobby. He had masses of information on the subject. He knew that Holly and Miranda couldn't understand why anybody should be fascinated by car numbers, and that was why they teased him about it. But it had been a hobby that had often helped their investigations in the past, and he knew that the two girls recognised that fact.

He led the way upstairs, to the Hamiltons' tiny spare room. This was the room the Mystery Kids used as their office.

'I was wondering if we should change our sign,' said Holly as she opened the door. The sign just had a single word: 'OFFICE.'

'To what?' asked Miranda.

'Something like "Control Room",' said Holly, opening the door. 'Like we saw at the police station.'

The three friends went inside. Although the room was small, they'd managed to squeeze in enough to make it look something like a real office. There as a chair and a small table. In one corner was a bean-bag Miranda used for serious thinking. On the wall was a huge map of London, with a clutch of coloured marker pins at its side.

As usual, Miranda dived straight for the bean-bag. ' "The Mystery Kids Control Room",' she said thoughtfully. 'Not bad. What do you think, Peter?'

'I think I prefer "Office",' said Peter. 'John Raven works from an office. And this looks more like an office than a control room.'

'True,' said Miranda. 'There aren't any TV screens in here, for a start.'

'Maybe you could bring your dad's computer up here, Peter,' said Holly.

'I don't think he'd be keen on that!' said Peter. 'Letting me use it is one thing, but snaffling it altogether is another!'

'Pity,' said Holly, sitting at the desk. ' "Control Room" has a nice ring to it.'

'A nice ring to it!' cried Miranda. 'That's it, Holly!'

'What are you on about?' said Holly, frowning.

'Ring!' said Miranda. 'That's what we need up here. A telephone! That control room at the police station was bulging with them.'

'Hmm,' said Peter. 'That's not a bad idea.'

'Why, do you have a telephone?'

'As a matter of fact, I do. It's an old one we had at our flat.' Peter and his father had lived in a flat when they first came to Highgate, before they moved to the house they were in.

'Hang on,' said Peter, disappearing through the door. Moments later he was back, carrying a rather battered telephone. 'There you go,' he said, putting it beside Holly on the desk. 'One control instrument!'

Holly picked up the receiver. 'Does it work?'

'I don't know,' said Peter. 'I took it to pieces once to see what was inside. I think I put it all back together again, but I'm not too sure.'

'There's only one way to see if it works,' said Miranda. 'Try it out.'

Peter picked up the dangling lead and

waved it above his head. 'It has to be connected, Miranda!'

'Then connect it, Peter.'

'To what?'

'To this, of course!'

Miranda had rolled over in the bean-bag and seemed to be trying to squeeze her head behind the small radiator that ran along the wall beside the desk.

Kneeling down beside her, Peter and Holly saw what Miranda was talking about. Attached to the wall, and tucked almost unseen into the corner where the radiator ended was a small white box.

'It's a telephone socket!' said Peter, surprised.

Holly laughed. 'That was well spotted, Miranda. Even somebody who's lived here for months might not have noticed it!'

'All right,' said Peter. 'But this desk was in here when we moved in, remember.' He grinned at Miranda. 'I'm just not in the habit of crawling round the floor like some people!'

'Well you can start now,' said Miranda, standing up and handing him the end of the telephone lead. 'How about plugging this in?'

Peter took the lead and dropped to his knees. Inching his way under the desk, he stretched to put the small plug into the connection box on the wall. Then, standing up again, he lifted the receiver on the telephone.

'A dialling tone!' he cried delightedly. 'It works!'

'One control room!' cried Holly.

'Not quite,' said Miranda, diving back on to the bean-bag. 'There's still one thing we haven't got in here that the real control room had.'

'What?' asked Holly.

'Cups of steaming liquid,' said Miranda. 'And biscuits. To keep us going.'

'OK,' laughed Peter. 'I get the message. Three hot chocolates coming up.'

As he ran downstairs to the kitchen, Holly's hand wandered towards the Mystery Kids' telephone, sitting proudly on the desk.

'I wonder if it *really* works?' she said. 'I mean, could we actually call somebody on it?'

'Or could somebody ring us?' said Miranda, getting to her feet. She hovered over the telephone, making brr-brring noises. After a couple of seconds she snatched up the receiver.

'Mystery Kids Control Room!' she said briskly. 'Mysteries and investigations our speciality! You name it, we'll solve it! Or find it! A runaway hippopotamus, you say? Just one moment, I'll hand you over to my colleague who runs the missing hippo department!'

Holly took the receiver from her. 'I see, madam. Your hippopotamus has been missing all day? Yes, of course we can solve that problem for you. No case is too big for the Mystery Kids!'

Holly just about managed to put the receiver back down again before she and Miranda collapsed in a fit of the giggles.

And that was when the telephone actually *did* ring.

The two girls jumped with surprise, Miranda letting out a little scream. They both looked at the telephone on the desk as if it were alive.

'The socket in this room must be an extension socket,' said Holly, whispering – although she wasn't quite sure why.

'What does that mean?' whispered Miranda.

25

'The phone downstairs will be ringing, too. When Peter picks that one up, this will stop.'

Miranda reached for the receiver. 'Oh, well. In that case we might as well save him the energy. It will be a good test!'

And before Holly had a chance to stop her, Miranda picked up the receiver.

Holly closed her eyes, waiting for Miranda to say something like 'Mystery Kids Control Room!' – or worse.

But Miranda didn't say a thing. As Holly heard a gruff, crackling voice, she opened her eyes again. Miranda had the receiver clamped to her ear and was looking thoroughly mystified.

'Pardon?' she heard her friend say.

Instantly the voice stopped.

'Hello?' said Miranda. 'Hello?'

The line had gone dead.

Miranda replaced the receiver as Peter pushed into the room carrying a tray with three mugs on it.

'Did either of you hear the phone ring?' he said, putting the tray down on the desk. 'I was sure I heard it go while I was in the kitchen, but by the time I came out it had stopped.'

'It did,' said Holly.

'It had,' said Miranda.

'What?'

'It *did* ring,' said Holly.

'And it *had* stopped,' said Miranda. 'I answered it.'

'You – what?' Peter looked at the phone. 'It works, you mean? Then – who was it?'

'I don't know,' said Miranda, shaking her head. 'A man. He didn't say who he was.'

Peter looked annoyed. 'You didn't ask?'

'I didn't get a chance to ask,' said Miranda. 'He started talking straight away. Anyway, it must have been a wrong number.'

'How do you know? Miranda, my dad won't be pleased if I've missed an important message.'

'You haven't. I'm sure it was a wrong number. What he said didn't make any sense at all.'

'Then what did he say?' said Peter.

'He said . . .' Miranda closed her eyes in concentration. ' "Falcon delivery confirmed. Friday at three. Top floor, as usual." '

'Falcon?' said Holly.

'Definitely.'

'What else did he say?' asked Peter.

'Nothing,' said Miranda. 'That was it. When I said "pardon", he hung up.'

Peter frowned. 'You're right. It doesn't sound as if it was for us. It must have been a wrong number.'

'There you are, then,' said Miranda, looking relieved. 'No harm done.'

Holly had reached for her notebook and pen as Miranda had recounted what she'd heard. Now, she looked again at what she'd written down.

'But it does make sense, Miranda, doesn't it? Listen. "Falcon delivery confirmed." That must mean that somebody called Falcon has ordered something from whoever was on the other end of the line. "Friday at three." That's when they're going to deliver whatever it is. At three o'clock in the afternoon.'

'Or three o'clock in the *moooorning*,' said Peter, lifting his arms and putting on an eerie voice. 'They might be delivering an illegally imported Transylvanian bat!'

Holly laughed, pleased that Peter no longer seemed to be annoyed. She read the last piece of what she'd written down. ' "Top floor as

28

usual." That's where they're delivering it to – the top floor of where this Falcon person works, I suppose. So it does make sense, Miranda.'

Miranda picked up her mug of hot chocolate. 'Then why did I say it didn't?' she said, frowning as she sipped.

'Well . . .' began Peter.

Miranda poked her tongue out at him. 'Read it again, Holly.'

'Falcon delivery confirmed. Friday at three. Top floor, as usual,'

'Top floor?' said Miranda.

'That's what you said.'

'He didn't say "top floor". There was some noise going on in the background and I didn't catch it properly. That's why I said "pardon". But I'm sure he didn't say "top floor".'

'Then what do you think he said?' asked Peter.

'Top something else,' said Miranda. 'Not "floor", but . . . "deck"! Yes, that was it: "top deck, as usual". *That's* why I thought it didn't make any sense!'

'Top deck, eh?' said Peter. He snapped

his fingers. 'Of course! You know what this means, Miranda?'

'What?' said Miranda.

'Boats have decks. This Falcon person isn't taking delivery of a Transylvanian bat at all. He's taking delivery of a Transylvanian battleship!'

Miranda started to hit Peter with a cushion. Then the telephone rang again.

The Diary

This time, it was Peter who stretched out and picked up the receiver.

'If it's a battleship salesman, tell them we don't need one!' hissed Miranda.

Peter waved an arm to quieten her down. 'Hello?' he said.

Holly and Miranda heard the voice crackle at the other end of the line.

'Mr Hamilton, please.'

'Mr Hamilton isn't here at the moment,' answered Peter. 'I'm his son. Can I take a message?'

The voice at the other end was interrupted by a loud noise, like a machine gun. It stopped almost as quickly as it started.

'Sorry,' said Peter. 'I didn't catch that.'

'Whittingham's Garage,' crackled the voice.

31

'Your father ordered a second-hand car from us.'

'Yes, that's right.'

'Well, it's ready for him. If he'd like to call in . . .'

Again, the man's voice was blotted out by the machine-gun noise.

'Sorry,' said Peter once more. 'I think there must be something wrong with this line.'

'I said if your father would like to call in at about four o'clock this afternoon, we can sort out the final arrangements and he can drive it away.'

'Oh, thanks!' said Peter. 'Thanks very much. I'll tell him as soon as he comes home.'

'Sounds like it's cruisemobile time this afternoon, Miranda,' Holly said as Peter put the receiver down.

'Certainly does, Holly,' said Miranda. 'Four o'clock, if I heard right. Four o'clock was it, Peter?'

Peter looked from Holly to Miranda and back again. 'Ye-es. Why?'

'Oh,' said Holly with a shrug. 'It's just that I haven't got anything terribly important to do this afternoon . . .'

'What a coincidence!' said Miranda at once. 'Me neither.'

'So I thought . . .'

'*We* thought . . .'

'We could join you. You know, cruising? Mystery Kids together?'

Peter shook his head and laughed. 'OK, I'll ask my dad if you can come along as well.'

Whittingham's Garage faced on to a bumpy side street, behind the main shopping thoroughfare. A row of rather tatty-looking coloured pennants, strung from two poles at either end of the forecourt, were fluttering in the breeze. Beneath them, each with a price in big bold numbers stuck across its windscreen, sat a collection of second-hand cars.

'Where is it?' said Peter, his eyes scanning the cars. He sounded anxious. 'I can't see it.'

'Is that it?' said Holly. 'Over there?'

A much newer version of Mr Hamilton's old car was parked by itself in the corner of the garage forecourt.

'Yes, that's it,' said Mr Hamilton.

'Su-per!' cried Miranda. 'And a whole lot cleaner than Guppy, Mr Hamilton!'

They crowded round the car. Although by no means new, it had been thoroughly cleaned and polished.

'I can see my face in it!' said Miranda.

Holly frowned jokingly. 'Hmm. Is that an advantage?'

A large, square-shouldered man arrived. He was wearing a rumpled shirt and a patterned tie which was loosened at the collar. He thrust out a hand towards Peter's father.

'Mr Hamilton! Good to see you again.'

Mr Hamilton shook his hand. 'Afternoon, Mr Whittingham.'

'Reg,' said the garage proprietor. 'Call me Reg.'

'Short for registration number, I expect!' whispered Miranda.

'All ready then, er . . . Reg?' said Mr Hamilton.

The garage proprietor nodded towards the gleaming car. 'Yes, all ready for you. Looks good, doesn't she?'

'She?' whispered Miranda loudly. '*She*? It's a car, not a girl!'

'Cars are always called "she",' said Peter.

He held up his hands as Miranda glared at him. 'Don't ask me why!'

'Come on, they're going!' said Holly.

Ahead of them Mr Hamilton and Reg Whittingham were walking towards the garage proprietor's office, a small glass-fronted room at the far side of the forecourt.

The three friends had just started to hurry after them when a loud rat-a-tat sound split the air.

'What's that?' said Miranda, stopping dead.

Peter tilted his head as the noise stopped, then started again for a moment. It seemed to be coming from behind Reg Whittingham's office.

'It's a drill or something,' said Peter. 'There must be a workshop behind the office somewhere. It was going on and off in the background when I took that call yesterday. That's why I thought the telephone line was faulty.'

Miranda looked at him as another short rat-a-tat burst sounded. 'You heard *that* sound on the phone?' she said.

'Why, Miranda?' asked Holly. 'What's wrong?'

Miranda shook her head. 'There's nothing *wrong*, exactly,' she said. 'It's just that . . . well, I'm pretty certain I heard that noise in the background of the call I took.'

'The one about the delivery for this Falcon person?' said Holly. 'Are you sure, Miranda?'

'I definitely heard something loud,' said Miranda. 'That's why I thought I'd misheard when whoever-it-was said they'd be delivering whatever-it-was to the top deck of wherever-it-was, if you see what I mean.'

Holly felt a little tingle of curiosity. There probably wasn't a mystery here – not a serious mystery, anyway – but the thought of solving the puzzle of the Falcon phone call was definitely intriguing.

Over in the corner, Mr Hamilton and Reg Whittingham had gone into the garage proprietor's office.

'How about a little wander round?' suggested Holly. 'Just a little one?'

Peter and Miranda smiled at each other. They both liked a mystery of any sort and they knew that Holly could smell one a mile away.

'Why not?' said Peter.

Moments later the three Mystery Kids were each taking their own separate route as they wandered, apparently aimlessly, between the cars for sale. Only when they'd gone past the small office and reached the corner of the forecourt did they meet up again.

'This way, I reckon,' said Peter as the rat-a-tat started up again.

Dodging down past a group of oil drums, they hurried round towards the back of the garage building. There they found a small rutted area, littered with rusting car parts and small towers of old tyres.

And, at the far end, an open set of double doors from which a loud noise suddenly burst. A rat-a-tat noise.

'It looks like a workshop,' said Peter. 'It's probably where they get the cars ready before they're handed over.'

'So what's making that noise?' asked Holly.

Peter and Miranda followed behind Holly as she inched closer to the open double doors.

Soon they could see into the workshop. A brown-overalled mechanic was working on a large and impressive-looking car. It was jacked up on stands.

'Whew!' whistled Peter. 'Some car!'

As they watched, the mechanic moved round to the side of the car. In his hand was what looked like an electric drill, connected to a socket on the wall by a curly red cable.

He bent down, and put the end to a nut on one of the wheels. Immediately the rat-a-tat noise burst out. Then again, and again as the mechanic removed all four nuts before lifting the car's wheel off.

'Of course,' said Peter. 'That's what the sound was. I should have recognised it. A wheel-nut remover.'

'Well I wouldn't have recognised it in a million years,' said Miranda. 'But I do now. And I'm certain it was the sound I heard.'

'Hey! You kids!'

The angry roar made them jump. The mechanic had put the wheel down and was moving towards them.

'Clear off!' he shouted.

'My father's buying a car,' said Peter, but the mechanic didn't want to know.

'I don't care! Get away from here! And don't come back!'

'Nice man,' said Holly as they scuttled round to the front of the garage again.

'Loud and smelly,' said Miranda. 'Just like cars, Holly! Perhaps they should be called "he" and not "she"!' She let out one of her loudest guffaws, rivalling the wheel-nut remover's rat-a-tat in volume.

Holly looked at Peter. He wasn't laughing. 'I don't think Peter agrees, Miranda. Do you, Peter?'

The question seemed to come as a surprise. 'Sorry,' he said, 'I wasn't listening. I was thinking about the car in that workshop.'

'Nice, wasn't it?' said Holly.

'Oh, yes. Super. But that wasn't what I was thinking.'

Holly looked at him. 'What, then?'

'I don't know. There was . . .' he shook his head, '. . . something about it. I can't put my finger on what it was.'

Mr Hamilton and Reg Whittingham were still in the glass-fronted office. The garage proprietor was sitting behind an old oak desk, Peter's father on the other side on a black leatherette chair that squeaked whenever he moved.

As the three friends crowded in, the telephone on Whittingham's desk rang. He snatched it up. A potential customer, thought Holly, as he answered the caller.

'No, I'm sorry madam. I don't have that particular model in stock at the moment. Yes, we do specialise in good-value cars. Top quality at a price yer purse can afford!' he trilled. 'If you care to give me your telephone number I'd be only too happy to call yer when we get something in . . .'

Whittingham picked up a pen and let his hand hover over the diary on his desk.

'Right . . . right. I've put it down against Friday. I fink I'll have something in by then, Mrs Murphy. Goodbye.'

Even though the desk diary was facing away from her, Holly could clearly read what Whittingham had just written: the caller's name, then her telephone number.

As the garage proprietor turned his attention back to Mr Hamilton, Holly's eyes wandered idly across the upside-down page of the open diary.

Suddenly, she spotted the name 'Hamilton'. Against it was the Hamilton's telephone

40

number. Holly recognised it at once. She looked at the day. Monday – yesterday. Reg Whittingham must put all his scheduled calls in this diary.

All his calls? Then . . .

Holly scanned the upside down pages again. Monday had only a few calls against it. The Hamiltons' and . . .

Above it was another number. But this didn't have a name against it, just the initial 'F'. Holly stared hard at the number, trying to commit it to memory.

Suddenly she was aware of Reg Whittingham looking at her. With a slam he shut his desk diary and stood up, his hand reaching out to shake Mr Hamilton's again.

'Well, it's been a pleasure to do business with you, Mr Hamilton,' he said. As Peter's father stood up, the garage proprietor quickly moved around his desk and ushered them all towards the door. 'Any problem with the car, just let me know and I'll have it fixed at once. Remember,' he said in his distinctive accent, 'quality and value, that's yer Whittingham promise . . . '

*　　　*　　　*

41

'Well, what do you think?' said Mr Hamilton, as he drove his new car away from the garage.

'Smashing,' said Miranda, from the back seat.

'Yes, really good,' said Holly, beside her.

'Good value, yer mean,' laughed Peter from the front. 'Quality and value, that's yer Whittingham promise!'

'Peter!' laughed Miranda. 'You sounded just like Reg Whittingham!'

'Did I?' said Peter. 'Yer really fink so?'

'Definitely,' said Miranda. 'Doesn't he, Holly?'

'Yes,' said Holly. But her mind was elsewhere.

'You don't sound too sure.'

'No, I do. Really,' said Holly, closing her eyes.

Miranda put a finger over her lips. 'Shh! Holly's trying to remember the route back again.'

But Holly wasn't. She was desperately trying to picture the page in Reg Whittingham's desk diary. In particular, she wanted to make sure she could remember the other phone number she'd seen – the phone number against which had been marked the single letter 'F'.

'F' for Falcon?

4 Who is 'Falcon'?

' "F" for Falcon?' said Miranda from the depths of the bean-bag on the floor of the Mystery Kids' office. 'You really think so?'

'Why not?' said Holly. She'd insisted on a meeting the moment they'd reached the Hamilton's house and had just finished explaining what she'd seen in Reg Whittingham's office. 'It was in his desk diary under Monday's date.'

'Yesterday. When you answered that peculiar call, Miranda,' nodded Peter.

Holly looked at him. 'It was written immediately above your phone number, Peter. Perhaps he was in a hurry and dialled your number by mistake instead of this Falcon person's number.'

Miranda looked up. 'OK, it's possible. The background noises were certainly similar. So what? What's the mystery?'

Holly shrugged. 'Only that we haven't worked out what that message meant.'

Holly slowly read from her notebook again. ' "Falcon delivery confirmed. Friday at three. Top deck, as usual." '

'Bit of a short message for Reg Whittingham, wasn't it?' said Miranda. 'I mean, he does go on a bit, doesn't he?'

'Yer right there, Miranda,' said Peter, mimicking the garage owner's voice perfectly.

They were right, thought Holly. It was a short message. But didn't that make it more suspicious? 'Perhaps he didn't want to be overheard,' she said, 'so he kept it as short as possible? Perhaps it was a secret message? Perhaps – perhaps it's in code?'

The bean-bag scrunched as Miranda rolled over on to her front and propped her head in her hands.

'It doesn't sound like a secret coded message to me, Holly. It sounds perfectly straightforward. A Mr Falcon is buying a car from Reg Whittingham's garage. It'll be delivered to him on Friday at three.'

'To a top deck?' said Peter. 'What does that mean?'

Miranda shrugged. 'Pass. But it's bound to be something completely normal.'

'You think so, Miranda?' said Holly, disappointed.

'Yes, I do,' said Miranda. 'Holly, I think you're looking for a mystery that just isn't there.'

Peter nodded slowly. 'I think Miranda's right, Holly. There didn't seem to be anything odd about that garage.'

'Nothing at all,' said Miranda. 'It sold cars, it had oily Reg to sell them, and it had a workshop round the back where the cars were got ready for oily Reg to sell.'

Holly couldn't argue. 'Just as you'd expect, then,' she said.

'Yes,' said Peter. He paused. 'Except that . . .'

Holly looked up sharply from her notebook. Peter had a habit of noticing things that most people missed. 'Except that what?'

'Except that,' Peter said slowly, 'I've just realised what was odd about the car we saw in that workshop at the back . . .'

'What about it?'

'It was a really expensive make.'

45

Miranda's head bobbed up again. 'So? What's odd about that? Some people buy expensive cars.'

'But not from Whittingam's Garage, they don't. The car in that workshop must have been worth at least five times as much as the most expensive one Reg Whittingham had for sale.'

Holly did the arithmetic quickly. It wasn't difficult. The Whittingham's Garage 'Car of the Week' had been in pride of place at the front of the forecourt, priced at £5995.

'Thirty thousand pounds?' she gasped. 'Do cars cost that much?'

'That model does,' said Peter. 'It was a Hewlett Sapphire.'

'A Hewlett Sapphire?' echoed Holly.

Furiously she began turning back the pages of her notebook. And there it was: jotted down after their tour of the police station.

'Look! The car reported stolen while we were in the Control Room. That was a Hewlett Sapphire.'

Peter came round the desk to look over one shoulder, while Miranda scrambled out from the bean-bag to look over her other shoulder.

'Numberplate N371 RWT,' Miranda read aloud. 'What was the number of the car at Whittingham's then? I didn't think to look.'

'Neither did I,' said Holly.

They both looked at Peter. If anybody would have noticed the numberplate, it would have been him. But Peter was shaking his head.

'I don't know . . .' he said. He even closed his eyes in an attempt to conjure up a picture in his mind, but it didn't work. 'No. I can't remember it at all.'

Holly's mind was racing. 'But if it was stolen – that could explain why that mechanic didn't want us around.'

Miranda pulled a clean sheet of paper from the desk drawer and spread it in front of Holly.

'Sounds like a new file, Holly, don't you think? "The Mystery of the Missing Motor"! How about that?'

Holly and Peter nodded in agreement. 'Perfect!' they said together.

Holly began to write in a heading, then stopped. She looked doubtful. 'Sergeant Hopgood said we shouldn't even think of looking for a gang of car thieves, remember?'

47

Peter nodded. 'True. But it's pretty unlikely that the Hewlett Sapphire we saw is the stolen Hewlett Sapphire, isn't it?'

'That's right!' said Miranda. 'Which means that it's also pretty unlikely we'll come across any car thieves to avoid!'

Holly beamed. 'But unless we investigate, we won't know!' she cried.

She pulled the sheet of notepaper towards her. ' "The Mystery of The Missing Motor",' she said as she wrote.

Peter and Miranda looked on as Holly carefully laid out in one place the things that they knew: the details of the stolen car, and of what they'd seen at Whittingham's Garage.

'Theory,' she said crisply. 'Whittingham's are dealing in stolen cars.'

'And selling them by telephone,' added Miranda. 'Put down the details of that phone call, Holly. Maybe this Falcon person is a customer!'

Holly jotted down the words of the mystery phone message to the equally mysterious Mr Falcon. She added the phone number she'd seen in Reg Whittingham's desk diary against the letter 'F', then drew a big question mark beside it.

'What's that for?' asked Miranda.

'Well, it is a pretty big unknown isn't it? We don't know for sure that it was Reg Whittingham who made that funny call. And, even if it was, we don't know that "F" stands for Falcon or that the telephone number I saw was the number he meant to call.'

'Sounds like a lot of ifs to me,' said Miranda.

'Well, here's another one,' said Peter. 'If that is a stolen car then you might be right, Miranda. Whittingham could have been letting this Falcon, whoever-he-is, know when it was being delivered.'

'So who is Falcon?' wrote Holly at the bottom of her notebook page. She underlined the question.

Suddenly, Peter dashed off downstairs. Moments later he was back again, a fat book in his hand.

'I know it's obvious,' said Peter, plopping the book down on the desk, 'but why don't we look in the telephone directory?'

Holly quickly riffled through the pages,

going more slowly as she reached the section she wanted.

'Falber, Falby, Falco, Falcoe . . . Falcon!' she said, jabbing her finger on the page. 'Three of them.'

As Peter read out the telephone numbers, Holly checked them against the number she'd copied from Reg Whittingham's desk diary. None of them matched. They weren't even close.

'He isn't listed,' said Holly.

'He could be ex-directory,' said Peter. 'You know, asked to have his number left out.'

Miranda shook her head gravely. 'That sounds suspicious to me. He's probably a crook. He wouldn't want an entry then, would he? I mean, "Mr Falcon, Stolen Car Purchaser", would give the game away, wouldn't it?'

'It doesn't have to be suspicious,' said Peter. 'People have their numbers left out of the directory for all sort of reasons.'

'Such as?'

'Such as if they don't want to be bothered by people selling things by phone,' said Peter.

'Maybe Falcon lives somewhere else in the

country,' said Miranda. 'He won't be in the London directory if he lives in Liverpool, will he?'

'No,' said Holly. 'But I don't think he does live outside London. Whittingham would have had to dial a different code to get his number if that was the case. He would have noticed if he'd found himself doing that.'

'So the fact that Falcon's not listed in the phone book doesn't prove a thing,' said Miranda with a sigh.

'It doesn't get us any nearer finding out who he is, either,' said Peter.

Miranda walked round the desk, stepping her fingers round the edge as she went.

'Of course there is one sure-fire way of finding out who he is,' said Miranda.

'How?' asked Holly.

Miranda's fingers continued tip-tapping until they reached the Mystery Kids' telephone. 'Call his number!' she said. And, before either Holly or Peter could do anything about it, she'd plucked up the receiver and was tapping in the number that Holly had seen in Whittingham's diary.

'Miranda! You can't!'

Miranda held up the receiver. 'I just have,' she said as the ringing from the other end sounded clearly.

Suddenly, it stopped. A man's loud voice said, 'Yes?'

Miranda quickly switched the receiver to her ear. 'Hello, Uncle Cedric! How are you!'

There was a brief pause before the man at the other end said clearly enough for Holly and Peter to hear, 'You got the wrong number, girlie.'

Miranda carried on. 'Come on, Uncle. I know you and your practical jokes! How are you?'

'Look. I said you got the wrong number.'

'Uncle Cedric!' laughed Miranda into the receiver. 'Stop it! How's the weather in Larkspur Rise?'

From the sound of his voice, the man at the other end was getting really irritated. 'For the last time, you got the wrong number.'

'You mean . . .' Miranda tried to sound totally embarrassed, '. . . you're not my Uncle Cedric? You don't live in Larkspur Rise?'

'Never heard of Larkspur Rise,' growled the

52

man. 'This is Beaumont –' He stopped talking, suddenly.

Miranda apologised, quickly. 'Oh, I am sorry. I really am, Mister . . .?'

She paused, hoping that the man would say his name. But all they heard was a dull click, and then the dialling tone came back again.

'Well, that didn't work!' said Miranda as she put the receiver back again. 'I was hoping he'd say his name.' She looked at the other two, still shaking their heads at her daring, and laughed. 'But at least we got an idea where he lives. Beaumont something.'

Holly got to her feet and went across to study their wall map. After a few seconds she reached for a red marker pin and jabbed it into a small road about three kilometres away. Red for mystery.

'Beaumont Crescent,' she said. 'That isn't too far. We could go there on the tube and have a look round.'

'Holly,' said Peter, 'we don't know that's the Beaumont he was talking about.'

Pulling an *A – Z of London* from the desk drawer, she flipped through to the index.

'Look,' he said, counting, 'there are twenty-three *Beaumont*s in London. It could be any one of them.'

Holly had to agree. Perhaps she should put red pins in all of them.

Peter was still talking. 'And we still don't know if the man Miranda just spoke to was called Falcon, do we?'

'No,' said Miranda. 'But we've proved it wasn't any of these.' She turned the telephone directory their way so that they could see the three Falcons listed. 'None of these live in Beaumont anything.'

'So,' sighed Holly. 'Where are we? The person Whittingham called with this mystery message might or might not be called Falcon . . .'

'And he might or might not live in Beaumont Crescent . . .' said Miranda.

'And he might or might not be receiving a stolen car from Whittingham's Garage,' said Peter.

The Mystery Kids looked at one another.

'Not short of mysteries, are we?' said Holly.

Miranda snorted. 'You can say that again!'

'So, what do we do now?' said Peter.

'First we need to find out if we are dealing with a stolen car,' said Holly decisively. She looked at her watch. 'It's six o'clock,' she said. 'What time does Whittingham's Garage close?'

'Six o'clock, Holly,' said Miranda. 'There was a sign on Reggie's office door.'

'Back to Whittingham's for another look round then?' said Peter, heading for the door.

Holly nodded. 'Yes. For a proper look round this time.'

 **Towed Away**

The small office at Whittingham's Garage was shut. A 'CLOSED' sign was hanging inside the door.

In the forecourt a couple were browsing amongst the cars for sale. Holly, Miranda and Peter watched them from the other side of the street, leaning casually against a lamp-post as if they were idly chatting.

'Do you know if there's a back way?' whispered Holly.

'I don't think so,' said Peter. 'Look, the garage backs on to the wall of that factory.' He pointed at the high brick building looming behind Whittingham's. 'The front way is the only way in.'

'I don't like it,' said Holly. 'Someone could see us.'

'We can duck down behind the cars, Holly,'

said Miranda. 'I mean, John Raven does it all the time.'

Miranda was right. Only last week, John Raven had managed to sneak through the carpark of a top-secret defence establishment without being spotted by one of the hundreds of guards on duty. The thought made Holly feel a bit better.

They had to wait for nearly ten minutes for the browsing couple to go.

'Ready?' said Peter, as the couple finally wandered off down the road.

Holly and Miranda looked from side to side together, as if they were watching tennis at Wimbledon. There was nobody else in sight.

'Ready,' whispered Miranda.

'Go!' hissed Holly.

Bending low, the Mystery Kids scuttled across the road and dived behind the first car on the forecourt. Then, with just the occasional bob up to make sure that all was still quiet, they crawled on hands and knees to the opening which led round to the workshop.

Holly leaned out for a final check, just in case the browsers had returned. They hadn't.

'Now!' she said.

Within moments they were round the corner and diving behind the piles of old tyres for cover. It was Peter who peered out from his pile first – and couldn't stop himself shouting in surprise.

'Guppy!'

Holly and Miranda looked over the top tyre of the pile.

There, parked in front of the workshop with its bonnet open, was Mr Hamilton's old car.

'What's it doing here?' said Holly.

'Waiting for the crusher-man to come and get it, I suppose,' said Miranda.

'Then why's the bonnet up?' said Peter. 'If they're selling it for scrap there's no point working on it.'

'I don't know!' said Miranda. 'You're the car expert. Searching for any decent bits they can take out, maybe? There must be something in it that still works.'

Peter shook his head. 'The car breakers will do that when they get it. That's how they make their money, by selling working parts and crushing the rest.'

Holly turned round to look at them. 'Can we discuss this later? I'm nervous enough as it is. Do we want to look in that workshop, or what?'

'Yes, we do,' said Peter, inching forward to her side.

Ahead, the workshop doors were closed tight. It didn't look as if anybody was there at all. Holly put her finger to her lips. They listened hard but heard nothing, only the sounds of their own breathing.

'Now!' whispered Holly.

Diving out from the piles of tyres the three friends scurried forward to the peeling workshop doors. They were firmly locked and bolted. Miranda stood on tiptoe to look inside.

The small, square windows in the workshop doors were covered in grime. It was almost impossible to see through them.

'It might help if they cleaned the windows now and again,' muttered Miranda. 'How can a spy expect to do any spying? It's a disgrace!'

'Maybe there are some more windows down the side that aren't so dirty,' whispered Holly. 'I'll go and see.'

'Do you know what to look for?' said Miranda.

'No.'

'Then I'll come with you,' she said, scurrying after Holly. 'I don't know what I'm looking for either!'

'Anything!' whispered Peter. 'Just make a note of anything you see. It might be important.' He began rubbing his arm across one of the windows in the workshop door. 'I'll see if I can make anything out here.'

The narrow gap at the side of the workshop led down to the solid wall of the factory they'd seen when they were outside. At the end it was overgrown with shrubbery, but for the first few metres it wasn't too bad. It wasn't too good either.

'Not exactly tidy, are they?' said Miranda as she found herself clambering over bits of rubble and assorted cans.

'No,' said Holly, untangling herself from a bramble growing out of the base of the workshop. She looked up. 'But the windows are a bit cleaner, Miranda!'

There were two long, narrow windows in the side of the workshop wall. Holly and Miranda took one each.

'Look,' said Miranda. 'It's the Hewson Emerald!'

'You mean Hewlett Sapphire,' hissed Holly.

'Whatever. It's still there.' Miranda put her nose right against the window. 'Isn't it?'

'Yes,' said Holly. 'I think. What's being done to it?'

The car in the workshop looked awful. Its windows and lights were covered in old newspaper, held in place by strips of yellow tape.

'Painting it, by the looks of things,' said Miranda.

Holly looked closer. Miranda was right. Every square millimetre of glass – windows, lights, mirrors – seemed to have been covered, presumably so as not to get marked by the new paint.

'But Peter said that's a new car, didn't he? Why paint a new car?'

Miranda didn't answer. Instead a look of panic suddenly crossed her face and she cried, 'Watch out!'

Holly spun round. Behind them, at the far end of the workshop area, the back of a truck was reversing round the corner and into the workshop yard.

'We've got to get out of sight!' yelled Holly.

But Miranda was ahead of her. 'Down here!' she whispered.

Holly followed as Miranda dived down to the overgrown shrubbery at the very end of the workshop. Plunging into it they discovered that there was a small gap between the end of the workshop and the factory wall. Breathing in as hard as they could, Miranda and Holly squeezed themselves in.

They were just in time. As they hid from view, the lorry turned the corner and began backing towards them. Holly caught a glimpse of the crane-like arm jutting out from the back of the lorry.

'What is it?' hissed Miranda.

'I think it's a breakdown truck,' replied Holly.

She risked another look out, peering along the length of the workshop wall. The truck had reversed in completely. It had a sign on the roof of the cab.

'Yes, it is,' whispered Holly, reading the sign. 'Rey Breakers. It must be here to pick up Mr Hamilton's old car.'

Even as she said it, the same thought flashed into each of the two girls' minds.

'Peter!' they exclaimed together.

'What if he's been caught?' said Holly.

For a moment, she felt panicky. What if Peter hadn't got away? What if he'd been spotted? Then, as she heard the sounds of the truck driver getting out of his cab and working normally, she breathed a sigh of relief.

'He must be hiding somewhere,' she said. 'We'd have heard the shouting otherwise.'

Miranda agreed. 'He probably nipped down the other side of the workshop.'

Holly looked past Miranda and along the narrow gap between the back of the workshop and the factory wall. It was completely blocked by odd bits of rubble and debris that had piled up over the years. There was no way they could get through to the other side to check.

'We'll just have to wait and see,' she whispered.

From the front of the workshop came a sharp clang. Then some more rattles and bumps. Finally, the truck's engine revved up.

'What's going on?' said Miranda.

Holly risked a look. Bending down low and leaning her head out slightly she could see the truck driver, half-in and half-out of his cab. He was looking backwards, towards Mr Hamilton's old car.

Of that, Holly could see no more than one of its front wheels. But it was enough. The wheel she could see was starting to move upwards.

'He's lifting up the front wheels,' said Holly.

'The cruncher-man, come for Guppy,' said Miranda. 'He's going to tow it away. All we've got to do is wait till he's gone.'

They didn't have long to wait.

When the front wheels of the Hamilton's old car had been raised about a half-metre from the ground the truck driver got out of his cab. Walking back, he seemed to check that all was well. Then, climbing back into the driving seat again, he slammed his door and began to move the truck slowly forward. Behind it, bonnet now shut tight and rolling on its rear wheels alone, Mr Hamilton's old car was slowly towed along. Moments later the truck had turned the corner at the end of the workshop area.

As the sound of its engine faded, Holly

and Miranda crept out from their hiding-place.

'Peter?' whispered Holly, as they stumbled out to the front of the workshop. There was no sign of him.

'Where are you?' called Miranda, hurrying across to look down the gap on the other side of the workshop.

She looked back at Holly. 'He's not here, Holly.'

'He must be!' Holly ran across to join Miranda. She saw at once that the gap on the other side of the workshop was even narrower and more overgrown with brambles. Peter couldn't have squeezed his way down there even if he'd wanted to.

'He must have hidden somewhere, Miranda! That driver would have seen him otherwise.'

'I know,' said Miranda. She looked around. 'But where? There was only his old Guppy here . . .'

'Oh, Miranda!' cried Holly. A sudden, awful, thought had struck her. 'He wouldn't have hidden in there?'

In her mind she heard the clang as if the

driver had shut a lid down. 'He has! He's been locked in the boot!'

'Holly, no!' gasped Miranda. 'The car's being taken to a breaker's yard. With one of those crusher things! He'll be crushed alive! We'll never see him again!'

'Sorry to disappoint you, Miranda . . .'

At the sound of that familiar voice, Holly and Miranda whirled round. A head, brown hair flopping over its eyes, was slowly emerging from the inside of one of the towers of tyres.

'. . . but I'm not going to be crushed or squashed! Not even squeezed! I'm here!'

At the sight of Peter climbing out of his hiding-place, Holly felt an enormous surge of relief.

'Peter Hamilton, don't you ever frighten us like that again!'

'Speak for yourself, Holly!' glared Miranda. 'That was a mean, low-down, rotten trick, Peter Hamilton. And I never want to see you again.'

Peter grinned. 'Make up your mind, Miranda. I thought you wanted to see me again!'

'Ohhh . . .' spluttered Miranda, before all three of them burst into relieved laughter.

Their mood quickly became serious again, though, as Peter said, 'Quick. Look at this.' Running across to the workshop door he peered through an almost-clean corner of one of the murky windows. 'Look. That's why I couldn't remember the number of this car.'

Holly took his place and peered through for herself. 'It's been taken off!' she said, looking at the blank space at the back of the Hewlett Sapphire where the numberplate should have been.

'Maybe it's still lying around,' said Miranda. 'Can you see anything, Holly?'

Holly squashed her eye closer. From this position she could just make out a small bench. It was directly beneath the side windows she and Miranda had looked through earlier, which was why they hadn't seen it.

And on this bench was a yellow numberplate!

'I think it's on the bench,' said Holly.

'Can you read it?' said Peter.

'Not all of it. It's got a rag or something on top of it.' Holly twisted her head round a bit further. 'I can read some of it, though.'

'What part?'

'Two of the letters. "R" . . . yes, and "W" And there's an "I" as well, before that.'

'An "I"?' said Peter. 'Let me see.'

He took Holly's place at the window. 'I don't think it's an "I", Holly. I think it's a "1".

Miranda was pacing up and down anxiously. 'Does it make a difference?'

'Yes, it does,' said Peter. 'Holly, what was the number of that stolen car?'

Holly thumbed back through the pages of her notebook. 'N371 RWT,' she said. Even as she read out the number her eyes widened. 'RW,' she repeated. 'And a 1?'

Peter was back at the window. 'If that rag's covering up the other parts of the number – then we've found it!'

'Hello,' said Holly into the telephone. 'Could I speak to Sergeant Hopgood please?'

The Mystery Kids had run all the way back to their office. Now, with Miranda and Peter standing anxiously at her side, Holly was about to solve the Mystery of the Missing Motor – less than a week after they'd first heard about it!

'Sergeant Hopgood speaking.'

Holly tried to compose herself, even though her knees were shaking with the excitement.

'Hello, this is Holly Adams. I'm with Miranda and Peter.'

'Yes, Holly. What can I do for you?'

'I – we—' stammered Holly, before her news came out in one big rush. 'That stolen car. The Hewlett Sapphire. We've found it. It's in a workshop at the back of Whittingham's Garage. It's being resprayed and the number-plate's on a bench . . .'

'Hold on, hold on.' Sergeant Hopgood sounded very calm. 'Where did you say you saw this car?'

'Whittingham's Garage. There's a workshop at the back.'

'A Hewlett Sapphire, you say?'

'Yes, that's right. One of the stolen cars was a Hewlett Sapphire, wasn't it?'

'Ye–es.' Holly frowned. Sergeant Hopgood sounded uncertain. 'You say you saw the stolen car's numberplate?'

Holly nodded furiously at the telephone as if it was Sergeant Hopgood himself. 'N371 RWT! Yes!'

'You're quite sure about that, now?'

'Yes! Well . . . no. We didn't see all the number. Just part of it.'

'Which part?'

'The "RW" part. And the "1" '

There was a long pause at the other end of the line. When Sergeant Hopgood spoke again, it was clear he was trying not to be unkind. 'Holly. Thank you for trying to help. But you're barking up the wrong tree, I'm afraid.'

Holly couldn't believe it. 'But – how?'

'Mr Whittingham drives a Hewlett Sapphire himself. I know, because he was involved in an accident last week. Somebody ran into the back of him. I think the car in that workshop is his.'

'The numberplate, though. What about the numberplate? We saw part of the stolen one.'

Sergeant Hopgood couldn't suppress a chuckle. 'No, you didn't. You didn't see part of a numberplate at all. You saw all of one.'

By the time Holly put the receiver down her face still hadn't stopped blushing.

'1RW,' she moaned softly, 'is Reg Whittingham's personalised numberplate.'

70

 **Diversion**

Miranda flopped down onto the bean-bag with a sigh. 'Well, that's the end of that mystery!' she said. She picked up the telephone directory and opened a page at random. 'I think I might have more fun reading this!'

Peter was shaking his head. 'I think Miranda's right, Holly. There is no mystery.'

Holly looked at him and nodded. 'I suppose so. Pity. When we got that wrong number message I really thought we might be on to something.'

Peter smiled. It took a lot to make Holly feel low. 'We could take a look round Whittingham's on Friday,' he said. 'It would be nice to find out what the message did mean.'

Holly brightened. 'Like's who's delivering what to where,' she said. 'We could pretend it was a coded message, and that the security of the country depends on our cracking it.'

Peter joined in, pleased that Holly was regaining her spirits. 'That's right. And that we're on the trail of a mysterious secret agent, code-named Falcon, known to be operating from a safe house in Beaumont wherever . . .'

'Crescent.'

It was Miranda. Submerged in the bean-bag, she was holding the telephone directory in the air.

'What?'

'Beaumont Crescent,' said Miranda. 'I'll bet a month's pocket money on it!'

Scrambling to her feet, Miranda plonked the directory down on the desk. But whereas Holly had expected her to have it opened at the "F" pages again – "F" for Falcon – it wasn't. Miranda was pointing at an entry in the "R" section.

'That truck, Holly. Remember the name?'

' "Rey" 'she said. ' "Rey Breakers" '.

'Right,' said Miranda. 'So what do you think of this?'

Miranda's finger was pointing at an entry on the page. In bold type it said, "P. Rey,

Car Breakers." The address was in Beaumont Crescent.

'It means,' said Peter, 'that Reg Whittingham called our number when he meant to call Rey Breakers. And when you rang the same number, that's who you spoke to.'

Holly pointed at the directory. 'But that isn't the number I copied from Whittingham's desk diary,' she said. 'It isn't the number Miranda called.'

'So they must have two telephone numbers,' said Peter. 'Some businesses do. It's not suspicious.'

'But using a code-name *is*,' said Miranda.

'What?' said Holly, wide-eyed.

' "Falcon delivery confirmed" – that was the first part of the message, wasn't it?'

'Yes,' said Peter. 'Delivery of an order to somebody called Falcon.'

'No!' cried Miranda. 'Delivery *by* somebody code-named Falcon!'

'You mean we've been reading the message all wrong?' said Holly. 'Whittingham was actually *calling* Falcon and arranging for him to deliver something on Friday?'

'Yes!' said Miranda. 'And Falcon is a big

ultra-suspect code-name!' She jabbed up and down with her finger on the telephone directory. 'Rey Breakers. *P. Rey*. P – R – E – Y. As in bird of prey. Get it?'

'As in a falcon,' breathed Holly.

Peter whistled. 'Looks like it's next stop Beaumont Crescent,' he said.

'Mind you, I don't know what we're expecting to find here,' said Miranda as they hopped off the underground train the next morning.

'Me neither,' said Holly. She had her notebook out all ready. 'But that's part of the fun of being a Mystery Kid, isn't it!'

Peter was already ahead of them, hopping on to the escalator rising up to ground level. They'd seen from their map that Beaumont Crescent was quite close to Tufnell Park station, only two stops down from Highgate, where they lived.

'It will be quicker by train than on our bikes,' Peter had said.

Miranda had agreed. 'And a lot less tiring! I don't think my legs were designed for bike-riding!'

The three friends stopped as they came out of

the station, blinking hard as their eyes adjusted from the gloom to the bright sunshine.

Peter checked the A – Z map they'd brought with them. 'This way,' he said, pointing to his left. 'It should be no more than five minutes from here.'

They started walking. It was a seedy area, with closed and shuttered shops and areas of waste ground. Suddenly, as they turned a corner, Peter said, 'There it is.'

The Mystery Kids looked at the street sign, high on the wall of a corner shop. At once it made their whole investigation seem much more real.

'Beaumont Crescent is only about 200 metres long,' said Peter, still looking down at the A – Z map. 'Rey Breakers shouldn't be hard to find.'

Slowly they moved along, feeling very conspicuous. 'Pretend we're looking for a house,' whispered Miranda, stopping to examine a list of names above a bell-push.

'So that somebody can come out and you can go through your Uncle Cedric routine again?' said Holly. 'No thank you, Miranda. Let's keep walking.'

'Rey Breakers!' said Peter. 'Look. Over there.'

They'd reached the top of the curve of Beaumont Crescent. Now they could see what had been hidden to them before. Ahead, just beyond a section of waste ground, was a large yard surrounded by a splintered wooden fence with 'Rey Breakers' white-washed on it.

Even without the name it would have been obvious that it was the place they were looking for. Above the level of the fence, old and rusting car shells were piled at least three high. From somewhere behind the fence they could hear the loud grating sound of a piece of heavy machinery at work.

'Don't tell me we're going in there!' said Miranda. 'If one of those cars falls on our heads none of us will get up again!'

'I don't think we'll need to,' said Holly as they strolled across the waste ground trying not to look suspicious themselves. 'Look at the state of that fence. There's gaps everywhere we can look through.'

By the time they'd reached the end of the fence they'd identified just the spot they wanted. A loose fence panel was hanging off conveniently close to a clump of bushes. Doubling back, the three of them ambled towards the bushes, then suddenly dived to the ground as they reached them. From the road, they couldn't be seen.

Carefully pulling back the loose fence panel, they looked through into the yard.

'There he is!' whispered Holly. 'Falcon!'

The same man they'd seen the day before, the man who'd driven the breakdown truck, had just emerged from a large corrugated garage no more than twenty metres away from them. The man was wearing a pair of paint-spattered overalls. Over his face was a white mask.

'What's he up to?' asked Miranda.

'Spray-painting something, by the look of it,' said Peter.

As they watched, the man went across the yard. The breakdown truck was parked in an empty space, Mr Hamilton's old car still dangling from the large hook at its back. He leaned into the truck, took something from under the dashboard, then went back into the garage again.

'We need to get a look in that garage,' said Holly suddenly.

'Why?' asked Peter.

'To see what he's doing. I mean, look around! If he is delivering something to Whittingham on Friday then that garage is the only place it can be!'

Miranda gazed through the gap in the fence at the piles of rusty wrecks around the yard. 'Not much doubt about that, I'd say. But do we have to go in there?'

'It won't take long,' said Peter. 'It's not as if we have to try to get in the front way. This fence looks old enough to . . .'

Gently he pushed his hand against the fence panel nearest to him.

'. . . come apart,' he said. With a gentle crack, the panel parted company with the bar holding it in place.

'Now all we need to do is think of a way of getting him out of that garage for a while,' said Holly.

'How about a diversion?' said Miranda.

Peter and Holly looked at her. 'What sort of diversion?' said Peter.

For some reason, Miranda was gazing into the sky. 'That sort of diversion.'

Holly shook her head. 'Miranda, I know I

shouldn't ask this, but what are you talking about?'

'We wondered if this place had two telephone numbers,' said Miranda. 'Well, it has. See!' She pointed upwards, at the wires stretching from a telegraph pole to their various destinations. 'Don't you have to have one wire-wotsit for every telephone number?'

'Yes, you do,' said Peter. He was looking up as well, now. 'And this place has got—'

'Two wire-wotsits!' cried Miranda.

Two separate wires came out from the telegraph pole towards Falcon's yard. One came down to end at the top of a short pole sticking up from the roof of the corrugated garage. The other seemed to end on the far side of the yard, at a low brick-built office just inside the yard's entrance.

'And I bet you,' said Miranda, 'that the number in the phone book is for that office. So how about me going to that telephone box we saw on the corner and ringing the Rey Breakers' number so that old Falcon over there has to leave his garage to go and answer it?'

Peter shook his head. 'I don't know, Miranda. It sounds risky to me.'

'Why? We want him out of that garage for a while, right?'

'Yes,' said Holly. 'But what if he doesn't answer it?'

'Then I'll keep on ringing until he does,' said Miranda. 'And when he does answer it, you two nip through the fence and have a look at what's going on in that garage.'

'But are you sure you can keep him talking for long enough?' said Holly doubtfully.

Miranda looked at her best friend in amazement. 'Holly Adams! This is me you're talking to, remember? Miranda Hunt, world telephone-talking record holder. Of course I can keep him talking.'

'What about?' asked Peter, still not convinced. 'Not the Uncle Cedric trick again, Miranda!'

'No, I'll just ask him to give me a few directions on how to get here from Highgate – then act a bit thick and ask him to repeat them a few times.'

'Act?' smiled Peter.

'Yes, act!' said Miranda. 'Now, do you want me to do it or not?'

Peter and Holly glanced at one another. 'We

shouldn't need more than a couple of minutes
. . .' said Peter.

'A couple of minutes?' said Miranda. 'No problem!'

'And if one of us keeps a look-out while the other checks that garage . . .' said Holly.

'Raising the alarm if worse comes to worst
. . .' said Peter.

'It should be OK.'

'Good,' said Miranda, moving away from the fence. 'That's settled then.'

She stuck up a thumb, John Raven-like. 'Give me a couple of minutes to get there.'

'And we'll meet you at the phone box after,' said Holly. She looked at Peter. 'OK?'

Peter nodded. 'OK.'

They watched as Miranda scurried along between the bushes and the fence until she reached the roadway. There, slinging her bag casually over her shoulder, she walked away whistling brightly.

As the sound faded, Holly and Peter looked at one another again.

'I wish she would learn,' said Peter, shaking his head. 'Why does she always whistle when she's trying not to be noticed?'

Holly shrugged, and she and Peter focused on Falcon once again.

'It's the waiting that's the worst,' said Holly a couple of minutes later.

She looked through the gap in the fence. Falcon was looking at Mr Hamilton's old car, still dangling from the back of his truck.

As he walked round towards the driver's door, Holly thought for one moment that he might be going to drive away. That would make life much easier! But, no. As he started the engine she realised that he was most probably just going to release Guppy and start dismantling it.

And then the phone in the Rey Breakers office rang.

On reaching the telephone box, Miranda checked her notebook for the umpteenth time. The last thing she wanted to do was call the wrong number – the one in the garage!

No, there it was, as she'd copied it from the phone book in the Mystery Kids' office: Rey Breakers.

Quickly she punched in the number on the

keypad, and heard the ringing signal through the earpiece. She waited . . .

Thirty seconds. Forty-five seconds. Miranda hung on, knowing it would take that long for Falcon to get across from the garage to the office.

One minute.

'Hello? Rey Breakers.'

Miranda recognised the gruff voice at once. Without a doubt it was the same man who'd answered her Uncle Cedric call.

'Oh, helloo,' she trilled, trying hard to sound years older. 'You buy cars do you?'

'For scrap,' said Falcon. 'Yes.'

'Ah. Good.'

'You got one? Give us your address and we can come and get it.'

'No, no,' said Miranda quickly, 'I will bring it to you. I think there's just enough life in the old girl to get her there safely. I'm going to miss old Bessie. Now then, my man, where exactly are you?'

'Beaumont Crescent,' said Falcon. 'You know it?'

'Ah . . . well . . .' hummed Miranda. 'Could you give me directions please?'

'You know the area?'

'Not very well.'

'Where do you know, then?'

Miranda had thought of the answer to this already. It had to be somewhere a reasonable distance away, but not ridiculous. Scotland was definitely out.

'Highgate Cemetery?' she said.

From the other end of the line came a deep sigh. Miranda could almost see Falcon closing his eyes and thinking, 'Women!' But, step by step, he began to go through the roads to take.

Miranda looked at her watch. Two minutes gone already. It was working! Holly and Peter must be in that garage by now. All she had to do was keep Falcon on the line for another three minutes or so . . .

'Got that?' said the gruff voice as he finished his list of directions.

'Er . . . oh, sorry. My pencil broke after the first one. It's OK, I've got a pen out now. Now, what was that again? Hello? Hello?'

There was no answer. The line had gone dead.

 **7 Memory Games**

As Falcon had stopped the truck engine and hurried across the yard to answer the office phone, Peter had pulled back the broken fence panel.

'Don't go until it stops ringing, Peter,' Holly whispered from behind him.

'I wasn't intending to!' said Peter.

They'd already agreed that Peter would go into the garage, since he was more likely than Holly to spot anything suspicious to do with cars. Holly was going to keep watch from the cover of the breakdown truck.

As Falcon answered Miranda's call, the loud ringing suddenly stopped.

'Go!' whispered Holly.

Ahead of her, Peter dived through the gap in the fence and scurried towards the garage.

Holly followed, pushing the broken fence panel aside to give her room to get through. Quickly, she ran towards the breakdown truck and crouched down.

No good! She couldn't see into the office properly. What she wanted was to make sure that Falcon was still talking to Miranda on the phone.

Keeping low, she crawled back towards Guppy. Perfect! By looking through the gap beneath the crane arm she could see Falcon talking animatedly.

Holly looked over towards the garage. Peter had agreed to come out in five minutes, no matter what.

The seconds ticked by. Time seemed to be crawling. Holly checked her watch. Two minutes. Just so long as Miranda could keep going . . .

And then, suddenly, the phone in the garage rang!

Desperately, Holly looked towards the office. Perhaps Falcon couldn't hear it. Perhaps he would ignore it. But, no. He had already slammed the office phone down and was coming out of the office door.

'Peter!' whispered Holly. 'Quick! He's coming!'

Inside the garage the phone was still ringing loudly.

'Peter!' Holly said again.

Suddenly she saw Peter's face. He was in the garage, hiding behind a stack of paint cans at the side. As she looked, he made a telephone sign to her by extending his thumb and little finger and holding it up to his ear.

She got the message. He wanted to stay and listen to Falcon's phone conversation.

'Oh, Peter,' Holly wanted to say, 'it's too dangerous.' But Peter was already tucking himself down into his hiding-place.

Holly had to get out herself, back through the gap in the fence. That was the arrangement. And she was going to have to do it now. Falcon was running towards her.

She turned – and felt her heart skip a beat. The broken fence panel they'd climbed through had slipped back into place. She couldn't tell where the gap was!

Holly's mind raced. She couldn't take the chance. Falcon would definitely see her if she didn't get the right one first time. No, she had to hide somewhere else. And there was only one possible place she could think of.

With a deep breath, Holly slid into the back seat of Mr Hamilton's old car and clicked the door shut.

In the garage, Peter tucked himself deep down behind the paint cans. Judging from the cobwebs and rust on them, they'd not been used in years. This had to be the safest hiding spot in here.

He knew he was taking a risk. But, from what he'd already seen Falcon doing in this garage, it was a chance worth taking. Besides, Holly knew where he was, and she would already be on her way back to find Miranda at the phone box. Together they'd do something if he were trapped.

There came the sound of running foot-steps, then Falcon's unmistakable voice as he snatched up the ringing telephone from the garage wall.

'Hello!'

Peter heard the faint and distorted voice at the other end of the line, but couldn't make out what it was saying. Clearly it was something that Falcon had been waiting for, though.

'And about time, too. I've got a Friday deadline, y'know.'

He paused briefly, as the voice at the other end said something.

'I know they're special. OK, OK. At least you've got them.'

The voice spoke again. Peter risked a peek out from his hiding-place to see Falcon shaking his head.

'No, I can't wait for you to deliver them. I'll come and get them myself.'

Falcon hardly gave the person at the other end time to respond before he snapped, 'No. Now. I'm on my way.'

And with that he slammed the phone down. The next thing Peter heard was the bang of a door and an engine being started. Carefully easing himself out from behind the paint cans, he crept across the garage and peered through a crack in the door.

'Whatever it is, he certainly wants it in a hurry,' Peter muttered as he watched Falcon drive out of the yard. The man was driving his breakdown truck.

And he hadn't even bothered to unhitch Guppy from the back.

Holly had never felt so frightened in all her life. As she heard the breakdown truck start up, then jerk forward, it was all she could do to stop herself screaming.

Wild thoughts flashed through her mind. She had to get out – but how? If she tried to open the door and scramble free, she could be killed. Even if the truck stopped, it could start again at any second. At least if she stayed where she was she'd still be in one piece when they finally did stop. Even if she was spotted then, the chances were that Falcon would be so surprised she'd be able to escape.

So what was happening? Why were they moving anyway?

Holly tried to piece together the information she had, to come up with some theory.

The call Falcon had received on his second phone must have been important – important enough for him to cut Miranda off and run across to take it. And why did he have two numbers, anyway? Why not just an extension, like the one they'd used in Peter's house?

90

Maybe, because he only wanted his other number known by certain people? The crooked people he was mixed up with, like Whittingham?

So if he was driving somewhere now, somewhere he wanted to get to so quickly he hadn't even unhitched this car from his breakdown truck, then it could be important to know where.

She had to see. She felt the truck stop. Then start again, swinging sharp left as it did so. As it began to speed up, Holly slowly inched across the back seat of Mr Hamilton's old car and lifted her head to the side window . . .

In the telephone box, Miranda was almost tearing her hair out. Falcon hanging up on her in mid-conversation had left her not knowing what to do. Should she hang up and ring again? No, he might come back at that very minute.

But then if he'd left the office, Holly and Peter would be in big trouble.

No, Miranda had decided. She had to hang on. Time went by. Two minutes. Three minutes.

'One more minute,' Miranda muttered as

she fed another coin into the slot. 'Then that's it.'

At that moment she saw the breakdown truck coming out of the yard, still towing Mr Hamilton's old car behind it.

'Well, no wonder he isn't talking to me!' said Miranda.

The truck approached. She shrank back into the corner of the telephone box, in case Falcon saw her. As the breakdown truck went past Miranda looked out – and found herself gazing straight at the stunned face of Holly, staring out from Guppy's back seat!

Not knowing what to do, Miranda numbly put the phone down. What was going on? Where was Peter?

That was answered quickly. As the break-down truck turned the corner and drove away, Peter came racing across the waste ground towards her.

'He's gone somewhere,' he gasped.

'I know,' said Miranda.

'To pick up something,' said Peter, breathless with both running and excitement. 'I heard him on the phone in that garage of his. I hid behind some paint cans. Holly saw me. Did she tell you?'

'What?' said Miranda, her mind still spinning.

'Holly. She got out through the fence and came back here to meet you.'

Only then did Peter see the look on Miranda's face. 'Didn't she?'

Miranda could only shake her head.

'Miranda!' shouted Peter. 'What's happened? Where is Holly?'

'In – in – ' stammered Miranda. Finally she forced the words out. 'In Guppy! I just saw her, as that truck went by. She mustn't have had time to reach the fence and jumped in there instead!'

Peter ran a desperate hand through his hair. 'Oh, Miranda. What are we going to do now?'

'Call the police, Peter. We've got to call the police. They can stop him.'

'But. . .' Peter said. 'I don't know where he's going! Only that he's picking up something.'

'Picking up something?' echoed Miranda. 'Not delivering?'

'No.'

'Then – then maybe he'll just go wherever he's going and come straight back?'

Peter saw what Miranda was getting at. 'So you think if Holly stays where she is he'll bring her back again?' said Peter. He looked at Miranda uncertainly. 'Will she have worked that out?'

Miranda gave him a steely look. 'If we've worked that out, then Holly certainly will,' she said.

'So what should we do?' asked Peter.

Miranda thought for a moment. 'Give them an hour,' she said finally. 'If they're not back here in an hour, then we call the police.'

After seeing Miranda out of the car window, Holly had ducked down again quickly. She knew that if she could see Miranda then Falcon might well be able to see her in the truck's rear-view mirror.

No, if she was going to be safe then she was going to have to keep herself tucked down on the floor all the way to wherever they were going.

Where Falcon was going could be important, though. If she couldn't see . . . could she remember? Would the memory trick she'd tried on their visit to the police station actually work? Could she even stand a chance of holding all the different numbers in her head? Holly doubted it.

As she shifted into a more comfortable position, something dug into her ribs. Reaching down, Holly pulled out her notebook from the pocket of her jeans. Of course! She might not be able to remember everything – but she could write it down!

Quickly, Holly began to jot down everything she could.

Since passing the telephone box they'd been travelling slowly for no more than thirty seconds. As the truck stopped, Holly wrote:

Slow 30

Holly checked her watch as the truck swung right and speeded up again. When it stopped again after a further thirty seconds she wrote:

Right fast 30

Listen! Smell! Holly kept on reminding herself of these things. She heard the sound of a pneumatic drill. Then she caught the delicious whiff of frying onions.

Drill – roadworks?
Cooking smell

As the truck came to a complete stop, Holly checked her watch again. Another sound made her write more:

Left slow, 20 stop
Bip-bip noise

Yet again, they set off before coming to a halt once more.

Ahead fast 30
Right slow, 15 stop

Holly held her breath, waiting for the truck to move off again. But it didn't. She heard the truck door slam as Falcon got out. They were there!

Briefly she thought about popping her head

up. But she abandoned the idea when she heard voices nearby.

'That them? All of them?' Falcon's voice, gruff and urgent.

'Yes, yes. Front, back and four sides.' A different voice, gasping a little as if he was speaking whilst doing something. Loading things on to the back of the truck by the sound of it.

Falcon spoke again. 'All numbered?'

'Yes. With the number you gave me.' The voice sounded irritated. 'I know what I'm doing.'

'Took your time, though.'

'Paul, I did 'em as fast as I could. These things have to be perfect or it shows. If they'd turned out the wrong size you'd have been back here fast enough.'

'All right, all right. Just so long as I can get 'em fitted before Friday. Whittingham will go spare otherwise.'

The next thing Holly heard was the truck door slam. Moments later she felt a movement. They were on their way again.

But where to?

*   *   *

'Ten minutes more,' said Miranda, looking at her watch for the umpteenth time, 'then we'll call the police.'

Peter nodded grimly. He'd been watching the road so much his eyes were starting to ache.

Miranda hadn't taken her eyes from her watch. 'Nine minutes and forty-five seconds more, then we . . .'

'There it is!'

The breakdown truck had just turned the corner and was coming towards them. Quickly, Peter and Miranda ran round the outside of the yard. Ducking down under the cover of the bushes they found the broken fence panel and pulled it back enough to see through.

Falcon drove into the yard and brought the truck to a halt. He started to climb out then, almost as if he'd just noticed Guppy for the first time, got back in again. Moments later, Peter's father's old car was being lowered to the ground. Falcon finally got out.

'He'll find her!' whispered Miranda.

'If she's still in there,' said Peter anxiously.

'She is! Look!'

Holly's face had appeared at the side window of the car. She knew exactly where she was. The timings and directions she noted since Falcon's stop were exactly the opposite of those she'd written down before. They just had to be back at Rey Breakers again.

Now she had to get out – and fast!

As Guppy bumped gently to the ground she risked a peek out of the window . . . and saw the broken panel in the fence swing open!

It was Peter! If she opened the door quickly and ran for it, she could be through before Falcon could do a thing about it. It would be better if he was taken by surprise, though.

As if answering her prayer, a sudden tremendous clatter came from the other side of the yard. Falcon looked up with a start. When another loud clatter came from exactly the same place, he set off to investigate.

It was the chance Holly needed. Opening Guppy's door, she slipped out.

'Quick!' said Peter.

Holly didn't need telling twice. Like a rabbit with an angry farmer on its tail, she shot across to the fence and dived through the gap.

'Thank goodness!' yelled Peter, giving her

a hug. 'This time I thought we'd never see *you* again!'

'The same goes for me!' said Holly.

'Can I stop throwing now?' said Miranda. 'Or shall I lob another one over?' She had a large lump of brick in her hand. Holly realised that this was the clatter Falcon had gone to investigate!

'Oh, Miranda!' cried Holly. 'Well done!'

'At least that's one diversion that's worked,' said Miranda. She dropped the brick and gave Holly a hug too. 'Welcome home!'

Holly grabbed her friends by the arms. 'Come on. We've got a lot of talking to do!'

8 Trackers

'So that's what happened,' said Holly, taking a deep swallow from the can she was holding.

They'd found a small cafe not far down the road and treated themselves to a soft drink each to recover from the strain of the past two hours.

'But you've got no idea what Falcon picked up?' asked Peter.

'No,' said Holly. 'But I think we're right about Falcon being a code-name. I heard him called Paul.'

'P for Paul,' said Miranda. 'As in P. Rey.'

'It would be good to know what he did pick up,' said Peter. 'It could be important evidence.'

'Peter Hamilton,' said Miranda, 'if you're going to suggest going back to that breaker's yard for another snoop around, forget it! I've gone right off diversions.'

'We don't need to go back there, Miranda,' said Peter. 'I saw all there was to see in that garage, I think.'

'What did you see?' asked Holly.

'A car. Being completely resprayed. A *new* car.'

'Not . . .'

Peter nodded. 'A Hewlett Sapphire,' he said.

'The stolen one?'

'I couldn't tell. They'd taken off the number-plates, and I didn't get a chance to look for them. I was just going to when that phone rang.'

'So you think that if we knew where Holly was taken it might give us some more clues?' said Miranda. Peter nodded.

'Well,' said Holly, fishing for her notebook, 'there might be a chance of finding the place again. A slim chance.'

'How?'

Holly opened her notebook and put it on the table. 'I couldn't risk Falcon seeing me, so I tried that trick of judging where we were going.' Miranda and Peter leaned in to look at the directions Holly had written down.

'So if we try to follow those instructions . . .' said Peter.

'We might find out where Falcon went?' said Holly. 'Yes. We'll have to adjust the times, as we'll be walking not driving.'

'Multiply by ten for somebody who walks as slowly as I do!' said Miranda.

'I wasn't thinking quite as much as that,' laughed Holly. 'But . . .' She looked at her first note: *Slow 30*. 'That's probably equal to about a minute's walking, don't you think?'

'And that,' said Peter, pointing at *Fast 30*, 'is probably more like three minutes.'

The Mystery Kids looked at one another. Without a word, they downed the remainder of their drinks.

'Let's go!' said Holly.

They began tracking from the telephone box Miranda had used.

'I started writing when I saw you, Miranda,' said Holly. She looked at the first of her notes: *Slow 30*.

'So it's about a minute or so in this direction,' she said.

They walked on until Peter, who was doing the timing, said 'Stop!'

'Now we turned right,' said Holly.

'There?' said Miranda, pointing. A little way ahead there was a right turn into a quiet side road. They crossed over and went that way.

'Now fast for thirty seconds,' said Holly. 'And I heard a drill or something.'

'About two or three minutes, then,' said Peter, checking his watch. 'Go.' They walked on until Peter said, 'Time up.'

'Nothing,' said Holly looking around. 'No sign of roadworks anywhere.'

'Hey!' It was Miranda, sniffing the air. 'Is that onions I smell, or is it onions?'

'Miranda,' said Holly. 'Is that all you can think about? Food?'

'Excuse me,' retorted Miranda. She tapped a finger on Holly's notebook, at the note beneath the roadworks mention. 'Cooking smell, you've written down there. And I smell one. It's coming from over there.'

Miranda pointed. A fast-food stall was operating on the other side of the road, its owner shovelling onions on to a hot-plate.

Holly sniffed the air herself now. 'Yes. That's it. That's the smell.' She looked around. 'So where are the roadworks?'

'There weren't any,' said Peter.

'But I was sure I heard a drill,' said Holly.

'You did. But they weren't roadworks. They were pavement works!' Peter was pointing himself now, at two workmen busy laying new paving stones. Beside them, on the ground, was the pneumatic drill they'd been using to dig up the old ones.

The Mystery Kids set off again. Following Holly's notes they took the next turning on the left.

'Bip-bip noise,' said Holly excitedly. Ahead of them there was a pelican crossing. 'We can't be far away now. "*Fast 30*",' she said, reading her notes, 'then turn right.'

They walked on, Peter counting off the seconds. When he stopped, there was only one right turn in sight. They crossed over the road.

'Fifteen seconds down here, and slower than slow,' said Holly, remembering the last part of the journey.

Peter counted. Finally he said, 'Here.'

'Here?'

Holly's spirits sank as she gazed about. They'd ended up outside a tiny clutch of shops. A newsagent's sat on the corner, a butcher's next door to it. On the other side of the road was a place that seemed to be selling mirrors of every description, its window full of them. On either side of that shop sat a hairdresser's and a pet shop.

'I must have got it wrong somehow,' said Holly.

Miranda shook her head. 'I don't think so, Holly. What about all the things we passed on the way? You got them right.'

Peter nodded. 'I agree with Miranda. Falcon must have come here.' He gazed about thoughtfully. 'The question is, why? What did Falcon say to the man he met, Holly?'

Holly checked her scribblings. 'Something about front, back and four sides.'

'Sounds like a haircut,' giggled Miranda. 'You're sure he didn't go into that hairdresser's?'

Holly laughed. 'And then checked to see how he looked in the mirror shop?' she said pointing at the window on the other side of the road. 'No, I don't think so.'

'The mirror shop,' said Peter. 'Of course! Front, back and four sides. That's where he must have gone! In there!'

'To get mirrors?' said Holly.

'Not mirrors,' said Peter. 'Glass! Front windscreen, rear windscreen and four windows!'

Miranda was shaking her head, mystified. 'Peter, you can call me a dimbo if you like,' she said, 'but don't cars come with perfectly good windows? Why have another lot made?'

'Because—'

'Peter,' interrupted Holly. 'Why don't we go back to the Mystery Kids office? This place is giving me the creeps.'

'Good idea,' said Peter. 'I'll explain it all there.'

'A car has a numberplate, right?' said Peter when they were back in their office.

'Right,' said Miranda. 'You haven't lost me yet.'

'Well, the same number is often etched on all the windows of a car.'

'Why?'

107

'To put off would-be car thieves. It's easy just to make up a new numberplate, but a lot harder to replace all the windows as well.'

Something occurred to Holly. 'So the chances are that only an organised gang would go to all that trouble? The sort of gang Sergeant Hopgood was talking about?'

'Yes,' said Peter. 'It costs money, too. So it's only worth doing for expensive cars.'

'Like a Hewlett Diamond,' said Miranda.

'Sapphire!' said Holly and Peter together.

'So this Falcon is in cahoots with the glass person,' said Holly. 'That seems pretty clear.'

'Yes,' nodded Peter. 'But Falcon looks like he could be the main man. He's the one doing the respraying . . .'

'Fitting new windows suppled by Mr Glass . . .' said Miranda.

'And then delivering the car to Reg Whittingham,' said Holly.

'Who's a car salesman!' cried Peter. 'And in a perfect position to come up with a customer! It all fits!'

'So . . .' said Holly. 'What do we do now?'

'Call Sergeant Hopgood?' suggested Peter, uncertainly.

From the depths of the bean-bag, Miranda gazed at the ceiling and started whistling.

'After the disaster with Reg Whittingham's car?' Holly shook her head. 'We would have to be absolutely certain this time.'

Peter looked at her. 'So what can we do?'

'Nothing,' sighed Miranda.

'But we've got to do something!' cried Holly.

'What?' said Miranda.

'That message said delivery confirmed for Friday,' said Holly. 'That's tomorrow. If only we could figure out where the handover is taking place we could go there. Then if we did see something happen we might think of something else we could do and if we did it . . .' She shook her head irritably as she realised what a jumble it all sounded. 'Oh, you know what I mean!'

The Mystery Kids sat and racked their brains. But thirty minutes later and after a round of raspberry milkshakes, they still hadn't come up with an answer.

'I think . . .' said Holly finally.

'What?' said Peter hopefully. 'Have you got an idea where this top deck could be?'

'No,' said Holly. 'I was going to say, I think we're just going to have to follow Falcon when he leaves his place.'

Miranda shook her head firmly. 'How? By wearing rocket boots? He'll be driving that car. Holly. The best we can do is to ride our bikes. We'll never keep up.'

'We could wait until he leaves, then get in *front* of him,' suggested Holly. 'If we rode three abreast he wouldn't be able to get past!' She wrinkled her nose. 'No, that wouldn't work.'

'Why not?' said Miranda. 'It sounded pretty good to me.'

'Because we wouldn't know which way to go, of course!' laughed Peter. 'You can't follow somebody from the front!'

Miranda flopped back into the bean-bag. 'You know,' she sighed, 'we've just been going round in circles on this one,' she said. 'Round and round and round and . . .'

Suddenly she sat bold upright. 'That's it! It must be! Yes! It must be! That's it! That's where it is!'

110

Holly looked at her best friend. Miranda had got excited in the past, but never quite as excited as this. 'Where, Miranda?'

'Round and round in circles!' shouted Miranda. 'A multi-storey carpark! And where do you end up?'

Peter's face lit up. 'On the top deck! Miranda, that could be it!'

Miranda's enthusiasm almost immediately sank a little. 'I don't know, though. Why should they hand over a car in a carpark?'

'I don't know either, Miranda,' said Holly, 'but the top deck of a carpark is the best idea we've had.'

'It's the only idea we've had,' said Peter. 'So it's got to be worth investigating. Well done, Miranda.'

'Yes, well done, Miranda,' echoed Holly scrambling to her feet to examine their wall map of London. 'Is that a carpark?' she asked, pointing at a blue diamond-shaped symbol with 'P' in the middle.

'Yes,' said Peter. He looked over her shoulder. 'There's one. And another one.' He sighed as he spotted a third. 'Three of them. What do we do? Take one each?'

Miranda shook her head. 'No. I vote we stay together.'

'I agree,' said Peter, looking at Holly. 'Getting separated is too nerve-wracking!'

'Then we're going to have to guess which one they're meeting in, aren't we?' said Miranda.

'Right,' said Peter. 'And yer better hope we get it right!'

As Peter slipped into his Reg Whittingham impersonation, Holly looked up sharply. It was her craziest idea yet. But . . .

'There is a way,' she said. 'Look. Those carparks are quite close together. We could get round all three of them in twenty minutes. So if we could make Falcon late for the meeting, half an hour late, say . . .'

'We could check the top decks of them all for a waiting Reg Whittingham? Is that what you're suggesting, Holly?'

Holly nodded, bright-eyed. 'Exactly! It's possible, but only if we can make Falcon late somehow.'

'And how do we do that?' said Peter. 'Ring him up and tell him the handover time has changed?'

Holly's reply nearly made him fall off his chair. 'Yes,' she said simply.

'What?'

'Peter, your Reg Whittingham impersonation is brilliant. If you rang up Falcon he wouldn't be able to tell the difference.'

'Come on!' cried Peter.

But Miranda was already reaching out to pick up the phone. 'Holly, you're right. Peter, it is a brilliant impersonation, honestly. You could do it.'

Peter gulped. 'But what if it doesn't work?'

'It can't fail,' insisted Holly. 'Put yourself in Falcon's position. Somebody sounding like Reg Whittingham calls him up on his private number telling him a secret meeting's been put back. Of course he'll think it's Whittingham!'

Hesitantly, Peter took the phone from Miranda. 'Are you sure?'

'Positive,' said Miranda. 'Tell him the meeting's put back to three-thirty, Peter. That will give us all the time we need.'

As she began punching in the telephone number, Peter had a sudden attack of stage fright. Impersonating somebody for fun was one thing, but doing it for real quite another!

'I can't do it!' he said as he heard the ringing sound start at the other end of the line.

'You can!' said Holly and Miranda together.

'No, honestly. I can't—'

But before Peter could put the receiver down, it was answered by the gruff voice of Falcon.

He had no choice. 'Falcon delivery on Friday,' he said, hoping desperately he sounded even a bit like Reg Whittingham. 'Now at three-thirty.'

'What?' growled the voice at the other end. 'What's going on, Reg?'

Peter's heart leapt. It was working!

'Change of plan,' he said into the receiver. 'Delivery at three-thirty. Yer got that?'

There was a pause. Then the voice at the other end growled, 'All right, half three. See you then.'

As the line went dead, Peter collapsed into a chair and punched the air at the same time. '*Yes!* He fell for it!'

The three Mystery Kids looked at one another excitedly. 'So far so good,' said Holly. 'Now all we've got to do is find the right carpark in time!'

 **Handover**

The Unicorn carpark was a grey brick affair, once voted the ugliest building in the country. It had four storeys and a basement. As Holly, Peter and Miranda arrived on their bikes they looked round for the pedestrian entrance.

'There,' said Holly, spotting a small door facing out on to the pavement.

Quickly chaining their bikes together, they went through the door and pounded up the flights of grey stairs. Signs on the wall told them how far they'd got.

'Level four,' gasped Miranda as they finally reached the top.

The three friends slowed to walk along the short passageway which led out on to the parking area.

'What if Reg Whittingham isn't coming himself?' said Holly, stopping suddenly. 'What if he's sending somebody else? We won't know what he looks like!'

'He'll be coming,' said Peter. 'Falcon said "see you then" when he was talking to me, remember?'

'All right, what if he recognises us?' said Holly, trying to think of everything that could possibly go wrong.

Miranda put on her most innocent expression. 'So? We're with Peter's dad and we've forgotten what his new car looks like. We're looking for it!'

And with that she marched forward and through the gap which led out on to the top deck of the carpark.

Holly and Peter followed – and saw at once that this wasn't the meeting place.

'It's almost empty,' said Holly, gazing out across the wide open area of tarmac.

Only a couple of cars were parked, and there was no sign of anybody standing around waiting.

'Five past three,' said Peter. 'They should have been here if this was the one.'

'Obviously it's not,' said Miranda. 'Perhaps none of them are.'

'We won't know unless we try them, Miranda,' said Peter.

'One down, two to go,' said Holly, heading for the stairs again.

Pedalling furiously across town, they reached the Lesley Street carpark in five minutes. This was a squatter building, much more modern.

'Can we take the lift this time?' Miranda panted as they chained their bikes up again.

'If they're working,' said Holly. She dived into the small pedestrian entrance and punched the lift button. The doors slid open almost at once.

They stepped into the lift and Peter pressed the button for the top floor. The doors began to close. Suddenly they sprang back again as a small woman wearing a smart coat and smelling heavily of perfume thrust her arm between them.

'Top floor for me, please,' she said as she got into the lift and the doors closed again.

The Mystery Kids glanced at one another. Could this be the one? Slowly the lift rose upwards until, with a gentle bump, it stopped and the doors slid open. The woman leapt out at once and ran off, her high heels clattering.

But she ran straight to a car parked near to the lift. She got in and drove off down the ramp which led to the ground.

'Never thought it was her for a minute,' said Miranda.

The part of the top floor they'd come out to was covered. There was no sign of anyone else. 'There's more this way,' said Peter, noticing an uncovered section to their left. They inched their way round.

'Look out!' hissed Holly.

A man in a smart suit was gazing away from them and out over the wall which bounded the carpark's top floor. Ducking behind a pillar, the three friends looked again.

'Reg Whittingham!' said Miranda. 'It's him, isn't it?'

'I don't know,' said Holly. 'It looks like him from the back.'

'Smart suit. Square head,' said Miranda.

'And he looks like he's waiting for somebody,' said Peter.

He certainly was. As the man continued looking down to the street, the Mystery Kids waited behind their pillar. Suddenly, away from them, they heard the lift doors open again followed by the sound of running footsteps.

Before they knew it a teenage boy had rushed past them. When he heard him coming the man turned round.

'Come on, son!' they heard him call. 'Your mother will be wondering where we've got to!'

'Oh, no!' cried Holly.

As they could see at once, it wasn't Reg Whittingham at all, just a man who'd looked very much like him from the back. What was more, they'd wasted five precious minutes watching him.

'Two down, one to go!' said Peter.

Holly gave a little groan. 'The last one. It would be.'

'Assuming it is the top deck of a carpark we're looking for,' said Miranda. 'I'm not so sure any more.'

'We'll soon find out,' said Holly, checking her watch. 'But only if we hurry. It's twenty past three. We've got just ten minutes to get there!'

*   *   *

Unchaining their bikes once again, the three friends raced off down the road. In the distance, ahead of them, loomed the third of the multi-storey carparks they'd identified.

Stowell Centre carpark was shaped like a cylinder, rising up from the ground to a height of five storeys. Its entrance was small, with just two striped barriers. Car drivers stopped at the first on their way in, to take a ticket from a machine. On their way out they stopped at the second barrier where they paid an attendant their parking fee.

It was almost half-past three as the Mystery Kids raced up to the front entrance.

'Quick!' panted Holly. 'We haven't much time!'

'You go on,' gasped Miranda as they dismounted. 'I'll chain the bikes up.'

As Holly and Peter raced off up the stairs, Miranda began looping their long chain through the rear wheels of the three bikes. She'd just finished and was about to head for the stairs when a loud voice yelled at her.

'Hey! You can't leave those bikes there!'

The miserable-looking carpark attendant

was leaning out of his cubicle and shouting at her.

'Why not?'

'Because this is a carpark, not a bike park, that's why! You're obstructing the public highway! Now move 'em! Before I call the police and have 'em moved!'

Miranda looked despairingly around. Move them? How was she going to lug three bikes somewhere else?

And then she saw it arrive – a Hewlett Sapphire car. As she gaped, wide-eyed, the man at the wheel of the car leant out and took a parking ticket from the machine. It was Falcon!

'Oi!' It was the sour carpark attendant again. 'What did I say about those bikes? You've got ten seconds!'

With a glint of red brake lights and a little squeal of tyres, the Hewlett Sapphire swept away into the darkness of the carpark.

As she saw it go, Miranda looked at the attendant.

'And then you'll call the police?'

'Too right, I will!' yelled the attendant.

'Really?' shouted Miranda.

'Yes, really!' roared the attendant.

'Go on, then!' shouted Miranda. 'I dare you!' And, leaving the three bikes just where they were, she raced off up the stairs.

Behind her, the attendant was so furious he didn't even notice that Miranda hadn't chained up the bikes. He simply reached for the telephone in his cubicle.

Holly and Peter saw Reg Whittingham as soon as they reached the top deck of the carpark. He was pacing up and down, looking at his watch.

'He must be wondering where Falcon's got to,' gasped Peter, trying to get his breath back. 'He thinks he's thirty minutes late, remember.'

Holly nodded, too puffed out to speak after their dash up the stairs. She looked across at where the garage proprietor had now stopped and was talking to the man who was with him. He had fair, slicked-back hair and looked very angry.

'Who do you think that is?' she panted.

'The customer probably,' said Peter. 'The one he's providing the car for.'

They ducked down quickly as Reg Whitting-ham looked their way. They heard the other man's angry voice.

'Two more minutes, Whittingham. No more. Then I'm going.'

'No, Mr Mills. Don't go. He'll be here.' Whittingham was sounding anxious. 'I don't know what's happened to him.'

Holly glanced at Peter. 'Maybe we fooled Falcon too well,' she said. 'If he doesn't turn up soon—'

She stopped as the sound of squealing tyres came up from the floor below. Moments later, they saw what Miranda had seen down at the entrance: Falcon, driving the sparkling Hewlett Sapphire up the carpark ramp and on to the top deck.

Keeping down, Peter and Holly crept behind a couple of cars so that they could get closer.

'About time too,' they heard Reg Whitting-ham say. 'Where have you been?'

'Three-thirty, you said!' It was Falcon, slamming the door and getting out. The driver's window was still open from when he'd got his parking ticket from the machine.

'What?' Reg Whittingham was sounding angry too, now. 'When?'

'Yesterday. On the phone!'

Holly and Peter looked at each other. 'If they realise they've been fooled . . .' she began to say.

But the third man interrupted the conversation between Falcon and Whittingham. 'Are we doing business, or not?' he snapped.

Whittingham turned to him. 'Yes, of course we are. Have you got the money?'

The man dug into his inside pocket and pulled out a wad of banknotes. 'Cash,' he said. 'So, where's the documents? I want to be sure this car can't be traced.'

As Whittingham pulled some paper from his own pocket, the three men went into a huddle.

'Documents?' whispered Holly. 'What sort of documents?'

'Registration documents,' said Peter. 'The registration documents prove you own the car.

'How?'

'They have the owner's name and address on, together with details of the car. Things like its make, its new numberplate . . .'

Peter stopped as, for the first time, he took a look at the Hewlett's Sapphire's numberplate. 'Holly! Look at the numberplate! That proves it's a stolen car!'

Holly looked for herself – and saw exactly what Peter meant. It was conclusive proof.

It was at that moment that Miranda came puffing up the stairs. Holly waved her down. Miranda crawled towards them, still gasping with the effort of climbing five flights of stairs.

'Miranda. We know that car's stolen. Somebody's got to run and call Sergeant Hopgood.'

'But . . .' gasped Miranda. 'I've already—'

'You go, Holly,' whispered Peter before the out-of-breath Miranda could mention the carpark attendant. 'You're the fastest runner. Miranda and I will try to hold them up.'

As Holly scuttled across towards the stairs, dodging from one pillar to the next, Peter and Miranda looked at what the three men were doing. Money seemed to be changing hands. The man who'd been waiting with Reg Whittingham seemed satisfied.

'He's getting into the car,' said Miranda,

finally getting her breath back. 'What are we going to do?'

'I think,' Peter said slowly, 'I'm going to lose something.'

Getting up, he ducked between a couple of cars. Miranda followed him. Across from them there came the sound of an engine roaring into life. The man Whittingham had called Mr Mills had climbed into the Hewlett Sapphire and started it up.

'Lose something?' said Miranda. 'What? Where?'

Peter had reached the ramp which was the only way down. With a lopsided grin he said, 'Here!' and dropped to his hands and knees!

As she heard a squeal of tyres, Miranda looked across the carpark. The Hewlett Sapphire was moving, swinging round the pillars – and heading their way!

'Stop!' yelled Miranda, waving her arms wildly as the car thundered towards them. It screeched to a halt as the driver saw Peter crawling on the ground.

'What the hell are you doing, kid?' yelled Mills. 'Get out of the way!'

Peter looked up, but didn't move. 'I've just

dropped my favourite marble!' he shouted. 'It must be here somewhere. Don't run over it, please!'

'I said, get out of the way!'

'What's going on?'

Miranda turned. Reg Whittingham and Falcon were coming their way too, now. Whittingham looked from Peter to Miranda and back again. 'I know you two, don't I?' he growled.

'Mr Whittingham!' said Miranda. 'How nice to see you. Yes, Peter's dad bought a car from you, remember?'

As she said this, Miranda saw Whittingham's eyes flicker. She ploughed on. Every second longer would give the police more time to arrive.

'Well, call us idiots if you like but guess what? Mr Hamilton brought us shopping – and we've forgotten where he left the car. How stupid can you get!' squealed Miranda, giving them a loud laugh for good measure. 'Anyway, we were looking up here when . . .'

'When I dropped my favourite marble!' wailed Peter. 'It's a speckled sparkler and

I've had it for years! Can you help me look for it, please?'

'Come on,' growled Mills impatiently, revving the Sapphire's engine.

'Can you help, please?' said Miranda, running over to him.

Mills glared at her. 'Help? I'll help,' he snarled. Opening the door of the car he climbed out and marched over to Peter. Grabbing him by the shoulders he lifted him angrily off his feet and half-carried, half-shoved him out of the way.

Then, marching back to the Sapphire, he brushed Miranda aside and jumped in. Moments later he was roaring off down the ramp with a squeal of tyres while Whittingham and Falcon hurried across to the lifts.

'Phew! said Peter. 'Not a nice man! For a minute I thought he was going to run me over!' He brushed down his trousers. 'Still, at least we know for sure we've found a stolen car. Pity we've probably not given Holly enough time to call the police. That guy's going to be out of here in a few seconds.'

Miranda whistled cheerfully. 'Oh, I think

it's going to take him a bit longer to get away than that.'

'Why?' said Peter. Miranda was waving a slip of card. 'What's that?'

'His parking ticket,' said Miranda. 'While he was carrying you off the ramp, I took it out of his car. I don't think that attendant's in a mood to let him out of here without it. Anyway, I've a feeling he's already on to the police . . .'

'Then what are we waiting for?' yelled Peter. 'Let's go!'

Haring across the tarmac, they dived past the lift doors just as they were sliding shut. Without stopping, Peter slammed the flat of his hand against the call button. As the lift doors slid open again, they hared on down the stairs to the floor below.

Peter hit the call button on that floor, too. On every floor, in fact, so that the lift would stop at every floor on its journey to ground level.

'That should slow them down a bit in case they come after us on foot!' he shouted as they ran. 'Let's hope it's enough!'

 **No Exit!**

Holly had rushed down the stairs as fast as her legs would carry her. Luckily she'd found a telephone box just round the corner. Her conversation with Sergeant Hopgood at the police station had been very quick.

'You're absolutely sure this car is stolen?' he'd said.

'Yes, absolutely!' she cried. 'It's had its identity changed. We know it has!'

Sergeant Hopgood had sounded stern. 'How do you know?'

'Because . . .'

'OK,' said Sergeant Hopgood the instant Holly had told him. 'We're on the way.'

Now, as Holly raced back to the multi-storey carpark, she wondered how Peter and Miranda had got on. Surely whatever Peter

130

had had in mind wouldn't have been good enough to delay them for long.

But it had! As Holly ran round into the entrance area, she saw that the Hewlett Sapphire was just coming up to the exit barrier. Any minute now, and Mills would be out. The police weren't going to get here in time!

And then, amazingly, the car just sat there; the barrier stayed down, blocking its way. Voices were being raised.

'I haven't got my ticket, I tell you!' the Sapphire driver was yelling.

'No ticket, no exit!' shouted the attendant. 'Or else you pay the full twenty-four-hour rate. Twenty pounds!'

In the car Mills was searching his pockets for money. Behind him a queue was building up.

'Holly! Did you call them?'

Holly swung round as Peter and Miranda raced down the stairs and out on to the pavement.

'Yes!' said Holly. 'They should be here any minute. What's going on?'

'Miranda took his carpark ticket,' laughed Peter.

'Oh, no!' cried Miranda. 'He's letting him through!'

Over by the attendant's cubicle Mills had handed over a twenty-pound note. The attendant was about to raise the striped barrier.

'Here they are!' shouted Holly.

'They?' said Peter. 'You mean "he", don't you?'

A single policeman had arrived on foot and was marching toward the carpark attendant's booth. The attendant hadn't lifted the barrier yet. Instead he was mouthing something to the policeman and gesturing angrily towards the Mystery Kids' bikes, still leaning against the wall where Miranda had left them.

'This isn't your policeman,' said Miranda. 'That's my policeman! Old sour-puss must have called him like he said he would!'

'It doesn't matter whose policeman he is!' shouted Peter. 'Quick, let's tell him!'

The Mystery Kids raced across just as the striped barrier began to lift.

'Stop!' screamed Holly, pointing at the Hewlett Sapphire. 'That man's driving a stolen car!'

As the policeman heard Holly shout he

turned to look at Mills, still waiting impatiently at the barrier. It was enough. Panicking, Mills shot the car forward. As he did so the barrier snapped in half – and jammed underneath the car's wheels. Mills couldn't control it. Seconds later the Hewlett Sapphire had smacked into the metal post at the side of the barrier and stopped dead, steam gushing out from its front.

Mills leapt out. As he tried to make a run for it, the policeman went after him and brought him crashing to the ground with a rugby tackle.

There was no time for congratulations. Over by the stairs the lift door was clattering open.

'We've got to stop them!' yelled Peter as Whittingham and Falcon, taking one startled look at the crumpled Hewlett Sapphire, began to lumber across the wide expanse of pavement alongside the carpark's wall.

As Peter dashed across to their bikes, Holly and Miranda followed. Moments later they were pedalling furiously across the pavement.

Peter reached them first, skidding round in

front of them so that Whittingham and Falcon had to stop dead to avoid having their feet run over.

The two crooks had no time to start running again before Holly did the same thing on her bike. Then Miranda, swooshing round in front of them with a cry of '*Whee!*'

'Get out of our way!' roared Whittingham, his head swivelling from side to side as Peter, Holly and Miranda flashed in front of them again and again as they rode round in a tight circle.

Suddenly Falcon made a dash for it. Leaping in front of Holly so that she had to brake sharply, he started to run – and then stopped almost immediately as a wailing police car shot round the corner.

'It's all up, Reg,' he said to Whittingham. He looked at Holly, Peter and Miranda with a scowl. 'Kids!'

It was all over very quickly, then. As Whittingham, Falcon and Mills were led to the police car, Sergeant Hopgood came over to the three Mystery Kids.

'Phew! That was close. Another minute and we might have lost them.'

'Thank you for believing us this time,' said Miranda.

Sergeant Hopgood smiled. 'I could hardly not believe you when Holly told me. What a mistake to make!'

'Tangling with the Mystery Kids, you mean?' said Miranda. 'I couldn't agree more!'

'She doesn't know yet,' said Peter as Holly gave Miranda a look. 'I didn't have time to tell her.'

'Tell me what?' said Miranda.

'The thing that clinched it,' said Holly. 'The one piece of evidence that absolutely proved they'd changed the identity of that car.'

'What?' said Miranda. 'Tell me!'

'Look at that numberplate,' said Peter.

Miranda looked over at the Hewlett Sapphire, still blocking the carpark exit. 'Oh no,' she giggled as she saw the numberplate with GUP as its three letters. 'Guppy's number!'

'Yes!'

'The crooks had chosen to swap the stolen car's identity for one that the Mystery Kids knew only too well.

For Guppy – Peter's father's old car!

* * *

'Well done,' said Sergeant Hopgood when he visited the Hamiltons' house the next day to tell them the news of what had happened. 'Thanks to you we've managed to crack a highly professional stolen car operation.'

The Mystery Kids looked at one another proudly as Sergeant Hopgood went on. 'They'd been stealing to order.'

'How do you mean?' asked Holly.

'Quite simple,' said the policeman. 'If Whittingham met a likely customer, he'd suggest that he could get hold of a really expensive car . . .'

'Like a Hewlett Sapphire?' said Peter.

'Like a Hewlett Sapphire,' nodded Sergeant Hopgood, 'at a very good price, no questions asked. Then, if the customer took the bait, he would arrange for Falcon to steal one.'

'And Falcon's yard was just a cover?' asked Holly.

'Well, not exactly. Rey Breakers' is a legitimate business, and does quite well. But for Rey – Falcon as you call him – that wasn't enough. He saw that he was in a perfect position to make extra money by stealing cars and changing their identity for cars that he'd actually scrapped. He did most of the work, and the things he couldn't do . . .'

'Like making new windows with the new numberplate etched on them,' said Holly, shivering slightly as she remembered her trip behind the breaker's truck.

'. . . he had done by others.' Sergeant Hopgood nodded. 'A clever gang, and a clever scheme.'

Miranda laughed. 'Until they picked Guppy for a second life!'

Sergeant Hopgood laughed, too, as he got up to leave. 'You're right, Miranda. That wasn't very clever. Especially with you three around!'

'Another mystery solved,' Holly beamed as they waved Sergeant Hopgood goodbye.

'And all because of a wrong number,' said Miranda.

Peter said, 'It definitely turned out to be a wrong number for that gang, didn't it!'

'Talking of wrong numbers,' said Mr Hamilton, 'I've got a little mystery I wouldn't mind having the Mystery Kids solve.'

'Any time, Dad,' said Peter with a grin.

'No problem Mr H,' said Miranda, brightly.

'Just say the word,' said Holly, flicking to a new page in her notebook. 'What are the facts of the case?'

'The facts,' said Mr Hamilton, 'are that the telephone I was planning to bring to my office suddenly disappeared and suddenly *re*-appeared in *your* office – and I'd like to know why!'